THE HAPPINESS OF FATHER HAPPÉ

DEDICATION

to

Helen and Joe

The soul shows herself in the mouth almost like colour under glass. And what is laughter but scintillation of the soul's delight, that is, a gleam showing itself without, no otherwise than it exists within?

Dante, *Convivio.*

and to Mrs. Mary Hopkins, whose generosity played a large part in getting this book back into print.

The Happiness of
Father Happé

By
CECILY HALLECK

ST. AIDAN PRESS
Harpers Ferry, West Virginia

The Happiness of Father Happé

Copyright © 2012 St. Aidan Press.

First published in 1938 by P. J. Kenedy & Sons.

Typesetting, layout and cover design copyright 2012 St. Aidan Press.

ISBN-13: 978-0-9719-230-2-7
ISBN-10: 0-9719230-2-7

For more information, contact:
www.staidanpress.com
staidanpress@gmail.com

CONTENTS

My publishers ask me to write a preface to this book. I do not like prefaces. If an author has not made his meaning clear in what he has written, it is not much use his *writing to explain what he has written*. So I have nothing more to say about the sense of the book.

How did I come to write it? I have no idea. I don't mind admitting that I remember picking gentians one May morning on the Mont Cenis Pass, cramming into so long as it took a fierce official to fuss over passports, an eternity of contentment with a roadside trickle of glacier water and those blue trumpets blowing triumph above the flint. And drifting down towards Chambéry and Annecy through the Forest of Arques, passing proximity to the Grande Chartreuse, my thoughts drifted and filled some hollow of my mind, I suppose. Late that night, when the hotel was asleep, I stayed for a long time on my balcony, tasting an intense solitude, listening to the forlorn bell of a forgotten Protestant church, while the wind that came from the Alps across the Lake of Geneva and Annecy's quiet town, tossed the early roses against the house. Cobbles in the street, wisteria leaves round the parapet, were glistening and smelt of rain; these things I remember, but I do not remember thinking of the ideas that are now in this book.

And quite unconscious that I was bringing back such ideas, I left Savoie next day. It was only two or three years later, when I had to face the question of a new serial, that I found *Father Savinius Happé, O.S.F.C.*, complete in every detail, in the forefront of my mind.

I can only say in the words of those before a magistrate confronted with their confederate, that I never saw him before and I cannot explain it at all.

CECILY HALLACK

Chapter I

The Simplicity of Father Happé

IT IS GENERALLY SUPPOSED that Franciscans are cheerful, and unlike most popular notions, this one, in my experience, is accurate. The little Franciscan monastery at Shingle Bay on the south coast is an ugly, sunny landmark. It looks as though five or six cottages had had a collision, which time and some creepers had healed. The largest of the apparently runaway cottages is the church, and the rest of them house a few theological students, and some friars who are in charge of the parish. Ruling over the lot is the Father guardian, Father Matthew, whose laugh usually leads the rest as you may hear, if you happen to be passing at recreation time. Everyone in Shingle Bay, Catholic, Protestant, or pagan, likes him. Policemen, shop-keepers, ladies who let "Apartments" in the summer, the doctor and Mr. Forbes-Chippenham at the Manor would nod if you mentioned his name, and lay claim to know him very well indeed.

It would be safe to wager a large sum of money, that they would have been as astonished as was that young theologian Father Hilary, D.D., if they had been in his shoes, or rather sandals, on that morning in early December when, watching his Superior read his mail, he heard him give an immense groan and put his head in his hands. In fact, all he could think of for the moment was that the Catholic Church had been wound up and the Holy Father had gone out of business.

"B-b-but what in the world is it?" was all he could utter, the eloquence which was the pride of the community brought to nothing.

1

"Someone's dead?... Are you ill, Father Guardian?"

"Worse than that," was the dread response, and the hands in which the head was, scuffled its hair this way and that, as though searching for the best handful to begin tearing out.

"Not...not Mrs. Badger wanting to play the organ at the Guild meetings again?"

Father Guardian's head left his hands, but only to shake itself, and the hands raised themselves to heaven.

"Worse than *that*," he said, "The Provincial's thinking we can do with another to help with the parish, and he's sending us..."

"Not...?" began Father Hilary, who had an almost feminine ability of daring to think the very worst.

"Father Happy," said the Guardian, and going to the window threw it up, knowing they would both need air.

The sea-fog rushed in and swirled round them, like a *génie* come to gloat over their fate.

The Guardian slammed down the window again, and with a shiver that was only partially for the weather, went over to the microscopic fire in the archaic grate, and kicked the five pieces of coal to an extravagant blaze.

What was more, poking through the tin in which he kept postage stamps, he produced a couple of cigarettes, and, straightening the bends out of them, he handed the best of the two to Father Hilary.

"Light up," he said, "we need something for the nerves."

Now before you have any further thoughts on the uncharitableness of people in whom you would never suspect such a thing and the disedifying behaviour that goes on behind monastery walls if all were known—let me explain about Father Happy.

Of course that was not his name. It was actually Father Savinius. Father Savinius Happé. Ah, yes, I *do* mean to say *that* Savinius Happé—the great geologist and the man who wrote these two books on botany, one on beetles, five volumes on Etruscan civilisation, a monograph on two Alpine orchids and the last word on the

Father Happé

Waldensian heresy. But of course I have seen his photograph, and know what a round smiling face he has: dreaming eyes behind bent, steel spectacles, crooked nose, big mouth with a quirk of humour at one corner. Then was it fear lest the friary could not make such a great man sufficiently comfortable that dismayed the Guardian? I am quite sure it was not. Father Savinius was well known among his brethren for the extreme simplicity of his tastes. Was it a certain more or less understandable insularity which remembered that although Father Savinius had entered the English province of the Franciscan Order, having lived with his English mother at Camberwell Green from the age of twelve onwards, yet, born in Savoie and having passed his early years at the farm of his father's people, he could never master either the English grammar, nor its intonation? It was not that either. Franciscan houses of study contain a fine assortment of nationalities, and the Guardian himself spoke German and French and Italian and a little Spanish.

At this point I realise, that, like most explanations, this one has made things worse rather than better. You are convinced by now that there was something very wrong indeed with Father Savinius, despite his photograph.

Well, then, I shall not attempt any further explanation. I will simply say that, in his reply to the Provincial, Father Guardian said that he noted Father Savinius was arriving on the Saturday before the last Sunday in Advent, and that he would count on him to preach for the Sunday High Mass. He would do his best to make Father Savinius at home at Shingle Bay and to give him all the leisure that remained after his pastoral duties, so that he might continue his literary work.

No, I blame Father Guardian for nothing, except for the unguarded remark which was overheard by a young student and joyfully reported to the common-room. "Well, the parish will know the worst by noon on Sunday."

When one faces an audience, one is bound to notice certain people here and there — the girl with the red hat, the old man with the ear-trumpet, the boy eating sweets — who are landmarks in it. So, when one thinks of a parish, one is bound to have certain people in the forefront of one's mind. And I think that when he made that remark, Father Guardian was bound to have in mind such people as Doctor Deedle, Mr. and Mrs. Forbes-Chippingham, the Misses Brackett who kept the sweet-shop, the Lestranges who kept the Gift Shop, Mrs. Badger, Roger Campbell in his motor-chair (he lost both legs at Gallipoli), and the Gardens with their six children under ten.

It was Doctor Deedle who, coming from attending Brother Porter's sprained wrist, saw the notice on the church door, and told Mrs. Forbes-Chippingham when he met her in the post office, that she was in for a sermon about geology next Sunday.

But by Sunday morning, the news had gone round the village so many times that Doctor Deedle's conclusion, when he arrived late and found the church full, was that the village must have been suffering from a long suppressed desire for information about geology, until then unsuspected. Having heard from his wife, who had been at the eight o'clock Mass, he knew that, for many of the congregation, this was a second attendance.

But the fact was, there is very little happening in Shingle Bay in the winter, and curiosity gets up an appetite.

When Father Guardian retired after giving out the notices, and sat down in the sanctuary, his attitude, hands on knees, was more than liturgically correct: it expressed a resignation redolent of the ages of persecution.

The sacristy bell tinkled, curiosity tingled, and the congregation, turning their heads with what they hoped was justifiable respect, were touched to an immobility like that of Tibetan worshippers, who do not breathe. Beaming upon them was the well-known face of Father Savinius Happé, but trundling underneath it was his body, which the photographer had always omitted, because it was completely spherical. In fact, with the assistance of his surplice and hood, he looked exactly like a tennis ball emerging, with a smile, from a twist of brown paper.

It is doubtful if any other preacher could have missed the gasp which greeted the audience's realisation of the fact that this bouncing dwarf was Father Savinius of literary, botanical and antiquarian fame; but Father Savinius had been so interested in the world in which he found himself from the moment when he looked up from his wooden cradle and blinked at his father's beard, that he had not got so far as discovering himself. He was, in fact, the most unselfconscious person who ever knew his own name and his own sins and was otherwise *compos mentis.*

Far from being discountenanced, his smile broadened with every step to the pulpit. His crooked nose seemed to join forces with the quirk of his mouth, and his large gray eyes to widen, in an effort to keep his satisfaction within bounds.

And when, by means of the extra stage in the pulpit, he appeared over it, and with an unexpectedly thin hand made the sign of the cross as though it were an experiment, his first words came out resonantly.

"I," he said, "am Happé."

I have it on the evidence of the youngest student, that even Father Guardian's head jerked round like that of a marionette, and that, as for the congregation, you could have heard a pin drop.

Yet, without anything but satisfaction in his voice, Father Savinius went on:

"What else could I be?" And here he paused, and smiled round the church.

Someone in the front of the church swallowed and choked, but nobody else moved.

"I am *very, very* happy indeed," said Father Savinius, "to come to you so that I have time to keep with you, the feast of Christmas." And while his congregation began to come out of their trance with stirrings and glances grins exchanged between those who were young enough to like to have their ears deceive them, he continued. "My Provincial, who stands for me in the place of Divine Providence has sent me to join your pilgrimage to Bethlehem. You know, it is a steep ascent. To understand it, it is like we climb a mountain!" His voice was vibrant and he pointed above his head to the iron supports of the roof, but even the boys did not find it funny, for in his eyes was the memory of the Alps, and they, who had never seen anything higher than the South Downs, knew, nevertheless, that he was thinking of some great dignity.

Then came the words for which Father Guardian was waiting, for in the houses of the Order they were a by-word.

"If we are to understand, we must be very simple. How God became a Babe, it is the great Mystery. I think I tell you a little story."

Father Guardian bent his head; and not one of his flock took it for a gesture of anything but humble attention. As a matter of fact he was praying. "O Lord," he prayed, "don't let him tell one of his worst!"

The Simplicity

"When I was a boy in Savoie," said Father Savinius, "my father had a mule. You know what a mule is like, *hein?* They are not easy to teach, isn't it? Well, and this mule of my father, we could not teach him. So my uncle, who is a priest, he say we shall call me Nescio, which means 'Know Nothing.'

"One day in the winter, when it was very cold, and when I was ten years old, I must take him to the mill for some flour. And we set out early because there was long to go and the darkness came down soon And we went troo the forest up and up by the little paths, up to the mill.

"When we turn back, it is already past two o'clock, and it is a dark afternoon. That was not very good. But much worse is Nescio. He will not keep to the path. I beat him, I back him, I talk with him, but when I am so tired that I am nearly in tears, for it was so cold, Nescio trows up his back heels, and he goes straight down the mountain, troo the trees, troo the thorns, over the rocks, troo the streams, and on his back I am beaten by all the branches, scratched by all the thorns, very much frightened and very, very cold, and I think that Nescio is mad."

There was not a boy in the church, nor anyone who had once been a boy, or knew how a boy feels, who was suffering from distractions. They had possibly forgotten that they were listening to a sermon, but they knew they were listening to a true story, told in a voice like a bell.

"And at last, when I was sobbing with the pain and with the fear, when it was very dark, there came the snow. It fell fast, in big flakes. I could not see the branches to push them aside, and so they struck me till I was fainting. And then, of a sudden, there were no branches, and Nescio's hoofs were on the road, and there was an open door, and I was in the arms of my uncle. I did not know anything more for a long while, and when I do, I was in a chair by the fire, and down the chimney there was coming the long flakes of snow of the greatest snowstorm that had been in Savoie for years.

There was not a boy
in the church — who
was suffering from distractions.

"My mother said to me then: 'We will not call him Nescio any more.' And my uncle said, when he came back from giving him a grand supper: 'Nescio knows just one thing: he knows what he needs and he flies from the darkness. He knew that great storm was coming.'"

Father Savinius paused and hunted in his sleeve for his handkerchief; but even when he produced it, with its hem half off and indications of pen-wiping on it, it did not distract his congregation.

"My children," he said, "what mules we are!"

He gazed affectionately at those he so apostrophised, and seemed to look at them one by one.

"We know nothing, and we are not easy to teach. We have what we call 'our own ideas.' We do not like if we are told we go the wrong way to work, isn't it? We are not simple, like the little donkeys who just stand by the Crib, and who learn to bear Our Lord to Jerusalem. We are stupid, not simple. We only know one thing. We know what we need, and we fly from the darkness, and so we save ourselves from the death of the soul. Good. It is a great thing to be not'ing more than we are. We will not ask to be the donkeys of the Lord, to be the donkey at Bethlehem, but only to come there, out of the darkness, because we need to be sheltered and to be fed. We shall not be hypocrites if we do that, for none of us," his gaze wandered over the pious and respectable congregation "is so bad that we are too bad to be a mule, or so ignorant that we do not know this need.

"And so," said Father Savinius, "we shall begin."

With which, he ended.

Chapter II

Father Happé, Communist

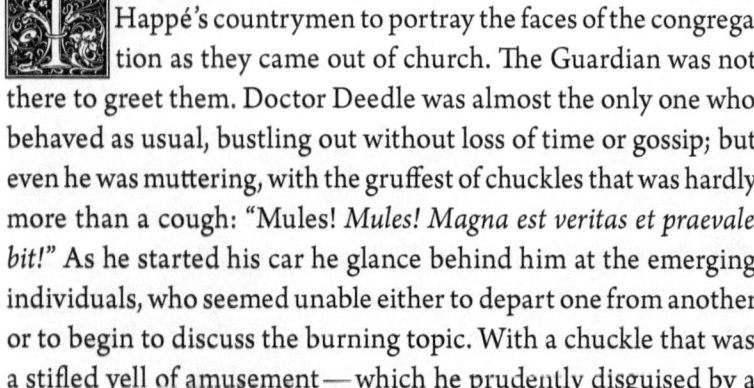IT WOULD HAVE TAKEN the mordant pen of one of Father Happé's countrymen to portray the faces of the congregation as they came out of church. The Guardian was not there to greet them. Doctor Deedle was almost the only one who behaved as usual, bustling out without loss of time or gossip; but even he was muttering, with the gruffest of chuckles that was hardly more than a cough: "Mules! *Mules! Magna est veritas et praevalebit!*" As he started his car he glance behind him at the emerging individuals, who seemed unable either to depart one from another or to begin to discuss the burning topic. With a chuckle that was a stifled yell of amusement—which he prudently disguised by a clashing of gears, Dr. Deedle drove off.

Mr. and Mrs. Forbes-Chippenham came out looking as though the frost had touched them. For Mrs. Badger, who dared to come in their way, Mrs. Forbes-Chippenham had only a word about the concert next week, further advances being made null and void by her anxiety that her husband should not stand in the cold. It was the first time for thirty years that Mrs. Forbes-Chippenham had implied the possibility of her husband's infringing her prerogative of delicate health; and, stupefied by it, he got into the motor before her without arguing.

What with the cold and congested emotions, Mrs. Badger's countenance was purple as it rose over the fur collar of her coat to support a hat that was a monument of respectability and provincial millinery. On the strength of the fact that her late husband had left two hundred pounds to the monastery without asking her permission, but mindful only that St. Peter would know more about his business than his wife did, and that he would like to have one alms-deed to think of on his death-bed — Mrs. Badger considered herself the parish patroness. Having failed to hold down the Forbes-Chippenhams, she was lying in wait for the Misses Brackett.

Miss Cissy was the first to emerge. One would have thought she expected her fellow-creatures to turn into greyhounds and chase her, so unwillingly did she venture forth from any building. Mrs. Badger was on her before Miss Cissy had seen her.

"Well, now!" the captive was asked: "What did you think of that? Mules! Did you see his handkerchief? How Father Guardian, who with all his faults knows what is suitable or ought to, dared put up a foreigner to preach when he knows English about as much as I know..." she was going to say French, but remembered that she had once been to Paris for five days, and said: "Eskimo!"

Miss Cissy tittered; but Mrs. Badger was not satisfied. It seemed to her a non-committal titter.

"Tcha!" said Mrs. Badger.

She was glad to welcome Miss Rachel, who joined her sister at that moment. The sisters were dressed alike, because Miss Rachel, who was five years older than Miss Cissy, fostered the hope that they were taken for twins. Unfortunately, they were dissimilar in everything else, and Miss Cissy's nervous movements bore no resemblance to the grace with which Miss Rachel appeared to be perpetually bowing to the inevitable with the upturned eye of ladylike regret.

"Oh, dear, oh, dear!" said Miss Rachel, bowing her unanimity with the feelings of Mrs. Badger.

"Have we gone mad?" demanded Mrs. Badger, knowing that Miss Rachel would not mistake her meaning that everyone save themselves were afflicted.

"I didn't know where to look!" said Miss Rachel, looking at heaven and laying the blame there as trustfully as usual.

"Mules!" said Mrs. Badger.

And there is no knowing what more she might not have said, had not Lois Lestrange and her husband Guy joined them.

"Yes, mules!" said Lois. "Isn't he marvellous? Ah, dear Savoie! I thought I was there! Guy, you must paint him! Who does he remind you of? He's pure seventeenth century!"

It is a pity that far from following Lois's train of thought to St. Francis of Sales, with his parables and fables, and the frank and original spiritual writers whose biographies the Abbé Bremond delighted to publish, Mrs. Badger could think of no one in the seventeenth century except Nell Gwyn. She had seen this lady on the films, and recalled that she was out-spoken and brazen.

"I'm sure that's a kind way of putting it," said Mrs. Badger.

Lois, who had short shrift for ladies who brought their disagreeable tongues to church, was about to be what her husband called "carbolic," when Roger Campbell's chair wheeled out of the door. He was talking to Mrs. Garden.

"A bit of fresh air, eh?" he was saying.

"The children loved it," said Myra Garden. "They understood every word."

At which, Mrs. Badger, unable to bear any more, but not daring to say what she felt to the present company, put up her umbrella as though she were hoisting a flag against rebels, and made off for home and dinner.

The topic had no chance to die down. By Tuesday, half the inhabitants of Shingle Bay had seen Father Savinius pushing its most notoriously disreputable perambulator — the property of a matron who called herself a Baptist on the strength of regular visits to the Baptist Mothers' Outing, and whose infant, certainly unbaptised, and in fact remarkable for his patient waiting for adult years (apparently) before undergoing any form of immersion in water, occupied one end of it, while the other was conveying a hundredweight of coal. By Thursday, Shingle Bay knew that Father Savinius had been knocked down by a bicycle and picked up by Alfred Webb and taken into Alfred Webb's flat to recover. The charitable hastened to point out that Father Savinius had probably hit his head on the curb and was too giddy to see at once that Alfred Webb was a Communist. But Mrs. Badger was of the unalterable opinion that the whole scene was staged to give Father Savinius an excuse to join forces with that Webb.

Neither school of thought imagined the scene that was actually taking place in the little flat above Higgs', the hairdresser's. The cheap curtains were drawn, and in one of the two deck chairs that stood on the rag rug before the fire and offered a semblance of bachelor armchair comfort, Father Savinius sat, drinking beer, with a rakish piece of sticking-plaster on his head.

From the other, Alfred Webb, similarly employed, regarded him.

"Well, how's that, comrade?" he asked.

"Very, very nice, comrade!" returned Father Savinius gratefully.

"Ha! Oh, that's funny! You didn't ought to call me that," said Mr. Webb, shaking his sandy head. "You're a borjoys, you are, and you got to choose between being set up against a wall and shot at, or comin' in with us straight!"

"Well," said the *bourgeois*, with a gesture of his mug, "I am in with you, am I not?"

"Ha!" said Mr. Webb, who liked his jokes simple, "That's very good. But it's not as easy as drinkin' beer!" He laughed at his neat reply, but then he regarded Father Savinius rather seriously. To tell the truth, he did not think it quite respectable for a priest to talk like this. He knew, of course, that all priests were hypocrites, but now that for the first time in his life he was talking to one, he was shocked to find him lost to all decency in admitting it.

"Ah, I know!" said Father Savinius, "I think I will smoke a pipe." He produced an ancient horror, and an old rubber pouch, from the corner of which he dug out a morsel of shag. "I know a comrade must have no private property. It all belongs to everyone. Will you have some of my tobacco?"

"That's the spirit!" said Alfred Webb, but with a glance at the shag, he added: "I don't feel like a pipe just now, thanks all the same."

"Ah," said Father Savinius, "no need to thank me. The tobacco is not mine any more than yours."

"Say," said Mr. Webb, leaning nearer, so that his deck-chair creaked ominously, "how long have you been thinking like this?"

"Fifty years," said Father Savinius.

"Cor!" said Mr. Webb, saving himself as the chair slipped on the linoleum. "Well, I'm scuppered! Wot was you — friend of Karl Marx, or something?"

"We were brothers!" said his guest, with a wide gesture. "But, poor Karl, he had not enough reason, not enough courage!"

"You mean to say you went further than 'im?"

"What's that noise?" said Father Savinius.

"It's all right. Shop's shut down below. Nobody can't listen in. Safe as the grave."

"But that cry!"

"Lumme," said Mr. Webb, "that was only a kid!"

Father Savinius rose, laid down his pipe, went to the window and flung up the sash. He put his head out, and peered down into the winter gloom.

"Hi!" he called. "It's all right, my cabbage! Wait one moment!"

With an agile turn he had gone to the table on which was a plate containing oranges.

The next instant he was crying:

"Catch! Queek! Catch!" And the golden balls were flying into the dusk, visible by the light of the street lamp, as also was the

"That was only a kid!"

head and shoulders of Father Savinius against the lit background of Mr. Webb's room.

For a moment there was silence and stillness in the room, because Father Savinius was watching a child's astonishment cut short its troubles, and Mr. Webb was paralysed at the action of Karl Marx's superior.

Then, utterly unaware that he had been watched by those passing by, Father Savinius waved his hand, calling out:

"You see, you never know when something nice will happen," and then drew down the window, chuckling.

He returned to pick up his pipe, remarking:

"The little one did not know she had some oranges in this room."

"Er, no," said Mr. Webb, unable to restrain a glance at the cold flat plate which, a moment ago, had been piled with golden spheres.

"You see," said Father Savinius, listening with apparent pleasure to the vicious bubble of his sixpenny pipe, "The weak have need of many things, but the wise need few. If I were wiser, I should not need my pipe and my tobacco, but I am an old fool, and I love to see the smoke going up, a little blue stair of cloud leading nowhere. It is good to be an old fool in at least three or four things, so as to be free from the need of feeling strong. And then I have nothing that is my own property. Tomorrow, you come to my room and you take anything you like."

"But if it isn't yours…" began Mr. Webb, drowning in this abyss of communism.

"No," was the reply, "I don't even possess the rights to give it to you, but I can ask permission to do so, and then I can. It's only an arrangement to make sure that I have no private property—so that the things I use are not mine at all. But you come and see. There is a fine pair of red slippers, very warm. Ah, but I am a wretched old capitalist! Do you know what is my joke?"

"No," said the numbed Mr. Webb.

"That no one will take my spectacles, because no one but me can see troo them!"

"Ha-ha," said Mr. Webb politely.

"Is there a watch here?" asked Father Savinius.

The wretched Mr. Webb would have denied it, but alas, it was a large affair, clamped on his wrist like a handcuff.

"Come now," he began, "I think you are going too far..."

"Going too far?" queried Father Savinius, who had risen, and was looking round for his coat. "You mean the time is going too far? Is that an idiom? Ah, I shall never learn it! I thank my stars I speak an international language. Is it yet six?"

Mr. Webb glanced at his watch very quickly and shot his cuff over it without delay.

"Quarter to," he said, but did not sit down again.

Father Savinius absent-mindedly fingered the fringe of the tablecloth.

"Your voice is hoarse a little," he said. "I think you need oranges. I will fetch some from somewhere and bring them. I shan't be long."

He let go of the tablecloth and departed with a nod. Mr. Webb remained where he was, stricken with relief at still having his watch and tablecloth, and with wonder as to how Father Savinius was going to replace his oranges. He stood there, back to the bright little fire which warmed his spine, while down the street Father Savinius was speaking to the aged owner of a poor little fruit shop.

"My dear," he said to the crone, "I am begging for the love of God and for a poor man who needs some oranges. When I have any money I will bring it to you. But could you, tonight, give me some oranges for this poor soul?"

The old woman regarded him shrewdly and in silence. Their eyes met, and they understood each other, as do those who understand poverty.

"You see," confessed Father Savinius, "he had some, and I gave them away to a child who cried, and then I found he needed them more because he has not so much as the child to make him happy."

The old woman nodded. It was not what he said that she understood, for she was a tired old thing who saved herself by only listening to key-words and by pretending to be deaf. But she understood the old man's face: he was one of the protectors of the unhappy and he wanted oranges. Without a word she put five in a bag—five large ones, which she mechanically chose and felt with her blackened thumb—and these she handed to him.

"God bless you, mother," said Father Savinius. "God reward you. I will come back one day soon."

Three minutes later he was panting up the stairs, bag in hand.

"Here you are," he said. "I got large ones. Well, good evening, comrade. Come round to the monastery tomorrow or the next day and try on the slippers. My boots and my sandals are enough for me, and I've kicked them both into such a shape that no one else will want them." He chuckled.

"Goodbye—er—and thanks," said Mr. Webb, regarding the oranges as though he expected them to explode.

"Until the day, comrade!" said Father Savinius, saluting with both arms, fists clenched.

Mr. Webb clenched a fist and returned the salute, but beside Father Savinius's double one, it looked half-hearted.

While the misshapen boots clumped downstairs once more, Mr. Webb stood listening to their departure with the greatest relief. It was only when the outer door had slammed that he moved.

Then he turned to his fireside, regarding the grate and the tongs and the scuttle full of coal, the rug and the two chairs, then the table still complete with its cloth and the plate once more plump with oranges. His watch ticked in the silence as though it were wagging its tail at still being with its owner.

Three minutes later he was panting up the stairs, bag in hand. "Here you are," he said, "I got large ones"—

"Dangerous, that's wot 'e is," said Mr. Webb to himself, thinking of his savings-book, his clothes, his job at the garage.

He went out and turned the key in the door of his flat, and mounted the stairs again, savouring the security of possession.

He would have shot both bolts as well, could he have heard, as others heard, the return journey of Father Savinius. The road back to the monastery was a footpath beside the railway, but it went beside the back gardens of a row of houses. Fancying himself alone, Father Savinius lurched along, giving full rein to his laughter. And he laughed like a Savoyard, gusty bellows of joy at the fun and folly of human limitations. At such laughter, and Englishman — and goodness, still more an Englishwoman — looks askance. It is too blatant a confession of common human nature. There is only one explanation: the author of it has been drinking.

So Father Savinius returned to the monastery, leaving behind him two blazen trails of scandal to stretch, meet and combine — that he had gone to the house of Webb the Communist, whence he had thrown oranges out of the window, and had come lurching home making the night echo with his laughter.

While the village rang with it Father Savinius was at Vespers, standing in the cold little choir among the other communists of God.

Chapter III

The Unscrupulousness of Father Happé

Y CHRISTMAS EVE, the story of Father Happé's return to the monastery after his evening with Shingle Bay's only Communist had been round the village so often, and had been brought to Father Guardian's ears by so many people who "thought he ought to know," that he could only mark time by filling the pulpit himself at Midnight Mass and the Sunday within the octave.

Publicly, he explained that Father Happé was "foreign." He dared not mention the word French, because Shingle Bay believed that nation to have a moral code remarkable in its absence.

It was presumed that he had reproved Father Happé. He had indeed tried to explain to the little savant that to laugh aloud to yourself, in an English village, was considered evidence of drunkenness, but the impression this made on Father Happé was only that he must do all in his power to free them from this Calvinistic or Jansenistic state of mind. He made suggestions for keeping the Feast of St. Francis with fireworks and dancing in front of the church, and declared that if Father Hilary would play his fiddle, he would do his best to learn some English songs.

Father Guardian's blood ran cold as he realised the impossibility of making Father Happé understand the Anglo-Saxon mentality; but at the same time — by some physical miracle — his heart warmed as he looked at the old professor.

"Father Happé," he said, "you must teach your own brothers some of your simplicity first. It is hard for a Franciscan to be simple in the Anglo-Saxon world of the twentieth century."

"*Mon Dieu!*" said Father Savinius, bumping down on his knees. "It is I — who with all my permissions to study should know more of the people I have to evangelise. Please be patient with me and tell me what it is I do wrong."

Soon, even to the most captious, it was evident that Father Happé had been misjudged. For, after one highly nervous visit, made merely to prove to himself that he was not afraid of a lot of priests, Alfred Webb became a constant visitor to the Monastery. He would not accept the red slippers, but he borrowed the great Encyclical called "The Worker's Charter," and the Life of St. Francis, by Johannes Jorgensen, and some volumes of the *Summa*.

His little walnut of a mind expanded and grew strong on the sap of Catholic philosophy. His nervous "Ha-ha" ceased to be the façade of a laugh with nothing behind it, and became a roar of enjoyment at jokes in the refectory when he stayed to supper, and when he talked with Father Happé.

Then the children discovered Father Happé, and from that moment, what "Farver 'Appy" did and said was the titbit of juvenile conversation in the village. He would play games with them, take bunches of them for walks in the country, where he would show them the mysteries of buds, birds and beetles, and above all, he would tell them stories. Stories of his boyhood, of local saints of his own countryside, of Franciscan miracles. He was, in fact, declared to be "as good as the pitchers" — no light tribute from film fans.

Then the unhappy discovered him. He would listen to their tales of financial insecurity, of unhappiness at home, of aches and pains and fears, with so much tenderness that there was healing in his listening.

Even the wild hares came to St. Francis. Even Miss Cissy Brackett came to Father Happé.

"Good afternoon, Father," she said tremblingly, rising from the broken armchair in the parlour. "I am sorry to take up your time,

'What Father Happé
did or said was the
tit bit of juvenile
conversation.

but..." She had an errand that was an excuse — something about the Guild of St. Paschal, of which she and her sister were secretary and treasurer, respectively. This errand was soon done, but half an hour later Miss Cissy was still in the broken-down armchair, and Father Savinius was still listening to the faint, uneven trickle of her telling.

What Miss Cissy said was that she was afraid she was very bad compared to her sister Rachel. Rachel always knew what to do and say, and was always right. Rachel never thought of herself, always of others. Rachel was self-controlled, prudent, economical, patient, hard-working. In fact, Miss Cissy seemed unable to leave the topic of her sister's virtues, until with a sob, she began violently to accuse herself of being in every way the opposite of Miss Rachel, and to explain that, knowing this, it made her feel she ought not to go on dressing exactly like Miss Rachel; but that it made Miss Rachel very vexed when she suggested this. It was hard, Miss Cissy said with tears, to have to look just like Rachel, when one was really full of unkind thoughts, very selfish and extravagant and dreamy.

In desperation, the penitent looked Father Savinius full in the face, as a rabbit in a snare might look at an angel stooped over it.

She saw in that round and unangelic countenance, behind the crooked steel spectacles, an expression of such comprehension that her flushed cheeks grew for an instant more crimson, and then cooled, and her clenched hands opened like those of a child's in sleep. It was as though she had been making an explanation, with immense difficulty, in a foreign tongue, only to find her hearer was a compatriot.

"How well I understand!" said Father Happé. "My child, let me promise you I will help you, for I know well how you feel! Listen to me — here I am with fifteen brothers, and I have to dress like them, and inside my habit, I am a lazy old Savoyard, an old professor that forgets everything, that wastes paper and goes off into thoughts about beetles in the middle of Divine Office, just like a little boy!

And I get angry, and I want to alter the world when people do what I think is silly things, or good things in silly ways. And there I am — Father Savinius, one of the friars, dressed just like my good wise brothers! So!"

Having Miss Cissy's gaze fixed on him with sympathy, her head nodding with it like a china mandarin's, he went on:

"The great thing for you and me to do is to receive the sacraments with great faith, to pray well to St. Anthony for ourselves and for our brothers and sisters, and to do a little good work that will make up for our faults, isn't it? Now surely your sister has a special intention — something she needs very much?"

"Oh, yes," breathed Miss Cissy, "A china cabinet! You see, she has our grandmother's china tea service — fifty-six pieces, Coalport, and how often she has hoped to get a china cabinet very cheap in a sale, so that she could display it safely in our front room!"

"Very well!" said Father Happé, understanding that Miss Rachel wanted a china coalbox but not stopping to marvel at the wishes of women. "You begin to come to Mass every Tuesday until St. Anthony gives it to her. And then, the little good work will be that you visit with me St. Dunstan's Home for the Blind Soldiers at Sandhampton. Mrs. Garden has promised to take me every Saturday afternoon in 'er motor. And as a little act of humility, you will tell your good sister that I give you this for a little penance."

Miss Cissy was dazed at first; but then, reddening and whitening like some newly opened blossom, nodding and clearing her thin throat, clasping and unclasping her hands, she accepted the guidance of Father Happé.

"Thank you, Father. Yes...yes, I could manage Tuesdays, because Rachel only goes Wednesdays and Fridays. You see, one of us has to open the shop. I am sure Rachel will spare me on Saturdays. I am sure she will when I tell her why. She will be so glad that I have decided to try to be more like her." It was clear that Miss Cissy was not too sure of being spared on Saturdays.

"And now will you remember a message to your good sister? I want, please, that you ask her to come and see me. I have a good friend, Madame la Marquise de Tour St. Etienne, who lives now at Forest Lodge—that is not far, is it? She organises for the Red Cross. She wishes that I find a lady here to tell the village how to put on their gas-masks when the Germans, or the French, or the Irish, or the Italians, or the Eskimos puff the bad gas at us. It must be a lady very clever and prudent and calm. Is it not right that I should ask Miss Rachel?"

Half an hour later, Miss Rachel, hands to ears, greeted her sister in the parlour behind the shop, with:

"Cissy, Cissy! Will you never learn not to run? The way you shut the front door went through my head! What ever has kept you? You never think how anxious I am getting when you are out alone!"

Miss Cissy, having been as harmless as a dove for forty-five years, had become in an hour as wise as a serpent.

"Dear Rachel!" she said, falling back, "Shall I never learn? Oh, forgive me again and be as patient as ever! Truly, I came quickly because I have such a message for you! You know the lady who is a French Marquise at Forest Lodge? She wants someone to organise the Red Cross Defence in Shingle Bay, and she's a friend of Father Happé's, and she asked him, and he says it must be you!"

It was only much later in the evening that Miss Cissy, sitting at her sister's feet by the fire, confessed that Father Happé had said she must do something to make up for all the trouble she had been to her sister, and that she, too, must do a little good work. A little visiting with him and Mrs. Garden.

Her hands were clenched as she waited for the response. The habit of forty years was not to be broken easily, and Miss Rachel was capable of going to Father Happé and telling him that hospital visiting was too trying for her sensitive sister and of offering to take her place. But to Rachel, going in the train of Father Happé and Mrs. Garden offered little scope for her organising powers, whereas getting the whole of Shingle Bay, singlehanded, as it were, into gas-masks for the inspection of a French Marquise was worth doing. Besides, thought Miss Cissy, as the seconds passed in silence, if the worst came to the worst, would Rachel get past Father Happé? For the first time in her life, there arose in her shivering soul the warm belief that she had an invincible champion, though he might (added her undisciplined imagination) look just like Humpty-Dumpty.

"Well," said Miss Rachel, "it will be occupation for you when I am busy. And if you do just as you are told and no more, you can't do much harm. You must see it doesn't get on your nerves. And I do hope, dear child, that you will really try to be more responsible, for if I am to do as Father Happé wishes — and I should blame myself for ever if I refused what was so clearly asked of me — I shall hardly know where to turn!"

And so it came about that the sisters were no longer seen together, inseparable as cruets. Miss Rachel was seen, to the wonder of the village, driving backwards and forwards to Forest Lodge in the Tour St. Etienne Rolls Royce. And Miss Cissy was found alone behind the counter of the shop, and alone with Father Happé and Mrs. Garden, driving into Sandhampton in Mrs. Garden's happy-go-lucky conveyance.

Owing to half an hour's voluble French conversation on the telephone, Madame la Marquise had been told that not only must she revive all the Red Cross enthusiasm which she had forgotten since 1918, but that she must ante-date its revival, since Father Happé had only been able to secure her an invaluable helper by foretelling that it would be revived. Widow of a great diplomat, she needed no further instruction, and being rather blind and frequently at a loss for occupation, was quite content to plan some work for somebody else to do.

So Miss Rachel listened spell-bound to orders given in tinkling and exquisite English, emphasised by gestures of a pale brown hand decked with ancient diamonds: and stayed to tea and to listen to tales of the Great War and great generals and politicians and spies.

Meanwhile, the blind ex-service men at St. Dunstan's at Sandhampton, were listening to a delicate little voice reading the papers, or trilling with laughter at their jokes. Jokes that were old and stale among themselves convulsed Miss Cissy, and hidden well-springs of laughter bubbled up in rapturous applause. They would pretend to tell her "army stories," but with their own unfailing delicacy, would never bring the least tinge of distress to her voice. They could not see here thin colourless face. But sometimes, they felt her soft fingers as she handed them fruit or took the papers they wanted her to read to them.

She became a football expert, and would hazard her opinion on the result of matches with great seriousness.

There was one man, George Allen, who was a Catholic, and liked her to read a Catholic paper. And, one day, somehow Miss Cissy told him of her "Thirteen Tuesdays of St. Anthony," and of the request for a china cabinet for her sister Rachel who was so good to her.

"*You* are very good to *me*," said George Allen, in his slow voice, "I reckon I could make that cabinet, if you want it so much. You come down to the carpenter's shop with me, and see what the instructor'll have to say to it."

There is no use going on with the story. I don't know which is the best picture to finish it with. The wonderful china cabinet which had actually been made, every inch of it, by a blind man. Or the owner of it, in her Red Cross uniform (but not, of course, in a gas-mask). Or Father Happé, with his head on one side, looking at it and at her, and seeing them both through a haze because his spectacles were lost (they were on the top of his head) and his eyes were full of curious tears. Or Miss Cissy, standing at the altar receiving another Sacrament, dressed like nobody on earth but herself, because she was being changed into a married woman with a new house of her very own and a solid husband named George.

Chapter IV

The Agnosticism of Father Happé

FTER MISS CISSY'S WEDDING, Father Happé could not appear at any religious or social function nor so much as walk down the street, without causing a stir. It would be hard to say if he were more popular or more unpopular than before, but it is quite certain that he was never taken for granted. To see him come into the Ladies' Working Party was exactly like watching a new sheep dog put into a field full of sheep. They were not frightened of him, but they were apt to preserve an unnatural calm and to go on with their business with their eyes glued to him. You see, say what you like, he had taken Miss Cissy from under the very nose of Miss Rachel Brackett. He had caused Miss Cissy—the trembling, meek Miss Cissy—to vanish, leaving in her place a Mrs. George Allen, who went into the tobacconist's and bought tobacco for her husband, who went to the cinema with him in the evenings and giggled at the jokes with him in a way Miss Cissy would never have dreamed of doing. It is true he had compensated Miss Rachel with a uniform, a china cabinet and occasion to take tea with a French Marquise, but after forty years of having something to bully, Miss Rachel felt the loss of it more keenly than the pleasure of her acquisitions. Even those who sympathised with Miss Cissy and were pleased to see Miss Rachel bested, had no inclination to be bewitched and done out of their own small holdings of power or precedence.

But Father Guardian was beginning to enjoy himself. He liked nothing better than to make Father Happé take his place at the last minute when the parishioners least expected it, and to hear the result afterwards. He put this right with his own conscience by saying that Father Happé never did worse than surprise them, and that this could do no harm; and he was beginning to appreciate the fact that his excuse was a very good one, because, far from doing harm, Father Happé did a great deal of good.

As for Father Happé, it was all the same to him whether he was set to lecture to the students or baptise a baby or even take a letter to the post. Obedience was his shining white way to heaven, and as along as his feet were set on it, he was in peace.

So, one wet Wednesday afternoon, the Guardian called Father Happé into his cell, and asked him to go down at once and take the Working Party.

"*Take?*" queried Father Happé, who had learned some idioms lately. "Photograph them?"

"By all means, if you can get hold of a camera!" responded the Guardian, cheered by a mental photograph of the proceedings. "That's a fine idea. But what I meant was go down and be there, and talk to them, and say grace for them at tea—do what you can to make things cheerful."

"Certainly, Father Guardian," said Father Happé. "That is right. They do not have much cheerfulness. And the weather is so cold."

"I say," called the Guardian, after his obedient friar, "Don't have any wild notions! Remember, they are very easily shocked… They will expect you to talk about something edifying."

"I understand," said Father Savinius, nodding. "I know them by now, the poor ladies. You must not laugh—that is wrong. You must not drink wine—that is wrong. You must not make the great joke—that is wrong. You must not sing—that is wrong. Nobody would have invited them to the wedding at Cana. But I begin to understand what they like. I study them. And when I was chaplain to that home for the poor things that had spiders on their ceiling, I learnt the tact." With a final nod of great prudence, he departed.

He went to his cell and thought over his duty as seriously as though he had been called to entertain the General of the Order or prepare for death, since, to Father Happé, one duty was as important as another. First, of course, he would do as the Guardian said: he would take their photograph. He had just time to go round to the flat of his Communist friend, Alfred Webb, and borrow his camera.

So, into the peaceful fold of the Working Party, disturbed by nothing but the usual amount of muttered acrimoniousness between those who were cutting out and those who were machining, there arrived the spherical, positively bomb-like figure of Father Happé, armed with an old-fashioned camera on stilts.

"Good afternoon, ladies," he said cherubically. "Father Guardian begs you will allow your portraits to be taken altogether."

This—when the working party could get its breath—was greeted with cries of dismay and shyness, but rather distracted cries, since the question was, how to get a look at oneself in the foot-square mirror hanging in the cloakroom without becoming a target for accusations of vanity. Mrs. Garden cheerfully pulled out a mirror and glanced at herself in it, saying: "What a good thing I have just had my hair waved!" Actually she cared not a pin whether she was taken with her head tied up in a duster or glorified by her new hat, for she was far too happy to worry about anything but her husband's reckless driving and the children's colds. Miss Rachel smoothed her uniform, straightened her tie, and regarded Father Happé more complacently than she had done since Cissy's wedding, for there is no gainsaying the fact that a lady always looks majestic in a uniform among those who are in their second best afternoon frocks. Cissy, for instance, had grown fatter since her marriage, and her dress appeared to have shrunk; as for her hair, with the curls that George encouraged her to indulge in, it looked like nothing so much as that of a doll at a jumble sale. She signalled to her to do something to her hair, but Miss Cissy giggled and only rolled a curl round her finger. But there was no time to say anything more, for the business of arranging the chairs had begun, and Mrs. Badger must not have it all her own way.

Father Happé was delighted with the reception of his idea, and was too busy arranging his contraption on the stand, which was only too truly called collapsible, to notice the ladylike scrimmage. Therefore, when he took a sudden preliminary glance through the lens, he was horrified by what he saw—the glance shot by Mrs. Badger at Mrs. Tugg, who had taken the centre chair by mistake. Mrs. Tugg was nearly blind. She came to the Working Party because it was warm in there, and she believed she was helpful in standing still for garments to be tried on her. The Working Party believed in erring on the side of largeness, and Mrs. Tugg was certainly the right mannequin for African natives according to their ideas. Actually, she could have done as much for a hippopotamus, poor dear. She was the plainest and most obtuse of women, but with the acute hearing of the blind. And she had heard Mrs. Badger's muttered: "Mistake!" and had blushed the color of pickled cabbage.

Now this is the distressing part of the story. It is useless to make any excuse. Father Happé's virtues were simplicity, obedience and humility. They did not exclude a quick temper. He was, by nature, an old Savoyard, and though grace had made him an old Franciscan, it had not changed his nature. There broke over him a rage as sudden as a mountain storm. The next moment there was an explosion, a white flare, and the room was full of a reek of powder. He had taken the photograph.

"But we weren't ready!" burst forth the chorus.

"I wasn't even sitting down!"

"You were in front of me!"

"You had your back turned, dear!"

Father Happé emerged.

"Ah!" he said, "I can't think what made me do it! I touched the powder without thinking! Well, it was a snapshot in verity!

32

And snapshots are sometimes remarkable. But now I shall take another."

For his penance, he stooped under the black cloth and adjusted the lens and the plate until they were ready, and took them as they wished to be taken. But his mercurial spirits were low when he had done, and putting this down to fatigue, the ladies said he must have some tea and that they themselves would be glad of it.

While they were bustling round, clearing the trestle table of calico, Father Happé sat down beside Mrs. Tugg, who had picked up her knitting and was soothing her soul with it. She knew she couldn't help with cups and saucers, and she accepted her uselessness without making excuse.

"I'm sure," said Mrs. Badger, groaning under a tray of china, "I shall be glad to sit down. You rest, Mrs. Tugg. It is a tiring afternoon." She believed that Father Happé, being a mere man, would hear her words and Mrs. Tugg would get the meaning of them. But she forgot that Father Happé was a Frenchman and so a natural psychologist.

"You are tired, Father?" asked the blind woman.

"I think I am," said Father Happé.

"Nothing like a cup of tea," she said.

Father Happé glanced at her, for, in his own country, to find solace for such unkindness in a cup of infusion would be the suggestion of an artist drawing human life with acutest irony.

"But in your country, you do not drink tea very much," she went on, as he did not reply: "Do you miss your country?"

"Sometimes I miss it very much," he said, answering her like a child.

"Tell me what your mountains are like, so that I can picture them," she asked; and Father Happé knew she did so to comfort him.

So he began to speak of his village in the Maurienne near Modane, and the river Arc which rushes icily and turbulently over its boulders beside it; of the little gray houses on the mountainside, small as stone matchboxes thrown casually down at the foot of those Alps with their precipices and their snow-capped peaks. He talked of the great Pass, the Mont Cenis and of the forests. And, unhindered by his bad English, which became worse and worse as his subject enthralled him, he and the blind woman were there in Savoie when Miss Rachel said:

"Tea is ready, Father, if you will kindly say grace for us."

And then he was back in the room that smelt of calico and gas fire and buttered buns and a tea-urn.

He said grace; but conversation failed him. It was not the prospect of the inevitable indigestion which this dreadful English meal would cause him; it was the sheer *mal du pays*. Never in all his years in England had it struck him down like this: the desire for the scent of snow, of pines and firs, and to be talking like a human being to the wood-cutter and the school-master and the grocer, their speech as free from dissimulation as the mountain air was free of germs. His hand trembled as he held his cup, for the white cloth was foreign to it and Father Happé longed for the smooth wood of a cottage table.

Conversation, however, failed nobody else. Everyone talked pleasantly to make up for the flash of feeling that had been revealed by Father Happé in the flash of the limelight. Everybody was a little anxious about the plate on which he had taken that picture, and still more anxious that the others should not guess this. But when talk is anxious, it is apt to have sudden unanimous pauses. And it was to end one of these pauses that little Miss Perry, the dress-maker, who was as ingenuous as her pink cheeks and blue eyes suggested, drew Father Happé into the conversation—or rather, asked him to lead it, by saying:

"Father Happé, there are so many wonderful shrines in France: won't you tell us about some remarkable answers to prayer that have been granted there?"

Father Happé glanced up. Through his crooked spectacles, his eyes met the bright, innocent glance of Miss Perry.

"Why, my child," he said, consoled by that innocence and honouring it with a care-free response, "do you believe in answers to prayer?"

"Of course I do, Father," she laughed, determined not to be teased by the kind old man.

"Well, what do you mean by 'answers' to prayer? Do you mean that God hears our need or that God gives what we ask?"

"Why, that He gives what we ask, Father."

He shook his head.

Everyone was listening; and little Miss Perry, innocently liking her role as bear-leader, said gaily:

"You don't believe He gives what we ask?"

"No," said Father Savinius Happé. "I am an agnostic."

Miss Perry would have led the laughter; but there was none. Sincerity is recognisable. An appalled silence acknowledged it.

After a moment, Father Happé remembered his duty. He looked wearily round the Ladies' Working Meeting.

"You do not understand me?" he said without hope. "But your charity will not allow you to think I am a bad Catholic. No; I am only afraid of being a bad Catholic. I must not be insincere. It seems to me that, for some peoples, they have only to make a novena, and, presto! there is what they want. But God has not led me that way. I have never received what you call an-answer-to-prayer in all my life, except that I prayed to be a priest. I pray that people shall live, and they die. I pray that the sick shall go better, and they go much worse. I pray that the sinners shall be converted, and they are not, and I wonder why? I know it is not because God is not good enough. I think it is because I do not ask the right things. But then I think: is it not right to pray that the sick shall get well and the sinners be good? Then I think that I do not pray well enough. But does not God hear the prayer of poor sinners? Then I think that it is not good that God should do good in my way. And I do not know what is the best way for God to do good. That is what an 'agnostic' should mean: one who says he does not know. I only know that what He wills is the right way. Perhaps, for you, what you ask He will do, because He wills to do it in the same way as you want it. Perhaps it is His Will to please you so. But it is not His Will to please me. It is His Will that I should be pleased with His Will which I cannot understand."

"But, Father," said Mrs. Garden, "you do not any the less visit shrines if you can, and pray for graces there?"

"Ah, but no!" he returned with the quick response of the sensitive to any understanding of their mind. "No! I go the most I can! I pray for all that seems good to me to pray for!…" then his voice changed, his smile faded, and he said more peacefully, "But when I have done that, I like then to say to God: Do Your Will! Do Your Will! And I like to think that what He will do, I shall not understand, because, me, I have the brain of a little beetle, and He is the great God. And I think how wonderful it is that He made my brain to know Him and His Commandments and to understand them enough to save my soul—but that the rest is for heaven! And then," he went on, with another gesture which expressed a change of mental standpoint, "I see how much good is done by what seems to me to be mistakes, accidents, and the malice of sinners. This person means harm, and they do good. This person means to do one good, and they do not, but they do another."

"Well, you have done me good," said Mrs. Tugg, to the general surprise, for she never raised her voice at the meeting. "I always wondered why I didn't get answers to my prayers."

"My child," said Father Savinius, sweeping buns off a plate with the vigorous Savoyard gesture of his arm, "We live in little houses and it is good for us to know that our thoughts are not big enough for the mountains of God's mercy!"

It was Miss Rachel who asked Father Happé to say grace. He looked bewilderedly down the table and perceived that everyone had finished. He glanced at her, like a child who expected to be reprimanded, but her smile, if majestic, was kind.

"Ah, I have preached!" he said with a shrug.

"And done nobody any harm!" she said soundly.

"You are kind, but I meant to make you cheerful!" he said, looking a little less crushed.

"Well, well, supposing you play for us!" she suggested, pointing to an aged upright piano which stood in a corner as though it had been given a long punishment. "Father Happé, Father Guardian says you are a great musician."

Her tone was encouraging. She had no notion that her phrase was literally true.

He glanced at the punished piano and shuddered. One glance told him that the punishment it received weekly had been deserved and that by now it should be a death sentence. But revived by the thought of penance, he advanced towards it, and in a moment, with his mouth twisted at the noise, he was playing the wildest mazourka. He played Schubert, Schumann; he played Hungarian dances and French folk-tunes; and try as they might, they could not stitch, but had to watch the flying fingers. Suddenly, in the middle of flying trills and brilliant chords, the piano stool collapsed.

Harmony was beheaded by Bathos.

There was a general movement to help him. He had torn his habit on the stool, and hit his head on the side of the piano. Miss Rachel was as competent as the circumstances permitted—giving a generous sample, shall we say, of what her competency would be in an air-raid and a gas-attack. Poor Mrs. Tugg, tangled in her knitting wool, was only in time to pick up the breviary which had fallen off the chair beside him; and returning to her place, what should she do but stumble into the camera and send the stand crashing to the ground in an ominous sound of breaking glass.

There was a curious cordiality in the voices that consoled her. Even Mrs. Badger said: "Never mind, dear, you didn't do it on purpose!"

For all his dizziness and the growing lump on his head, Father Happé saw everything remarkably clearly. He saw in his mind's eye, that photograph which revealed faces anxious to find the best place and Mrs. Tugg blindly groping, and the bitter face of her accuser.

"Didn't she?" said Father Happé to himself, looking at the calm face of the clumsy, ugly woman whose prayers were not answered with many consolations any more than his own.

Father Happé began to laugh at himself.

"What a chapter of accidents!" said Mrs. Garden, laughing too.

Father Happé saw the slow, wise smile broadening on the face of Mrs. Tugg.

"Ah," he cried, "look what a queer way I have made you cheerful!"

But only his own soul—and perhaps Mrs. Tugg's?—knew how queer and long a way the answer to his prayer to do so had come.

Chapter V

The Appalling Utterance of Father Happé

ATHER HAPPÉ's terrible first sermon, his Communist activities and his statement that he was an agnostic were all matter for the gossips to shock themselves with, but thanks to the discretion of those who heard it, his worst utterance was only known to three men. Possibly it was only comprehended by two, because the person to whom it was addressed was already more than a little dazed.

It happened like this. One afternoon in early spring, when the birds were singing and the crocuses were golden, white and purple, Father Guardian sent for Father Happé and asked him to go down to the parlour and find out what a certain Father James Ellis wanted. Father Happé, newly come from the delights of a German geological quarterly, blinked at him, withdrew his mind with immense difficulty from the implications of some mathematical calculations about a cavern in the Andes, and went obediently, if not recollectedly, down to the parlour.

There, sitting on the edge of one of the horsehair chairs and entertained by nothing but the stencilled pattern on the once salmon-pink walls, sat a meagre cleric. To Father Happé he looked like one of those strange molluscs that are only known to the curators of the most uninteresting museums of natural science. As a matter of fact, at that moment, Father Happé's tide of attention was on the point of turning back to the cavern in South America, but there was just one thing that would always arrest his attention and bring it back from theories and books, and that was, if he was faced with an individual who looked cold. Whether this was because he had lived, in his youth, in that grey village under the Alpine peaks, and knew all about the snow that blocked the passes, or whether it was because he detested the chilliness of English houses and manners, I cannot say; but certainly he advanced on Father Ellis like a St. Bernard retrieving human life from a deep drift, and positively growling with sympathy at finding him left there in a fireless room, carried him off to his cell, where the central heating provided a modicum of warmth. Moreover, as Father Happé had just begun to write another book, he had been moved to a large cell and bidden by the Guardian to light the gas fire in it when he felt the need of it. Father Happé never felt anything when he was writing, so he had not been much of a charge to the community gas bill. Now he put a match to it with great satisfaction.

"There," he said, pushing his spectacles on to the top of his head and blowing his nose like a trumpet of exultation on a check duster which he had been using all day under the impression that it was his handkerchief, "now we have the English comfort! My dear Father, do you smoke?"

Father James Ellis was as paralysed by this gusty cordiality as though he had really been frozen and brought suddenly into a warm place. His face seemed stiff and he could hardly answer. He fumbled in a dazed kind of way for his pipe. He was even too stupid to stop himself saying:

"I haven't any tobacco."

Father Happé exulted even more, and hunting over his desk, dislodged a pile of books with a crash like an avalanche, and produced a tin.

"The Archbishop left it behind!" he said.

Father Ellis did not even take that in, but with a faint smile began mechanically to fill his pipe. But there were signs of returning animation. He sneezed. He lit his pipe. He drew a long breath, and then he took the pipe out of his mouth, conscious of his manners.

"You are most kind, Father," he said. "You must forgive me. I am absent-minded..."

Father Happé chuckled.

"Then we shall indeed be sympathetic!" he said

Father Ellis shook his head.

"The circumstances are very different," he said. "Absentmindedness is the privilege of a great scholar. It is a great honour. I had no idea I should have this privilege."

Father Happé was looking extremely uncomfortable.

"You will please not say like that," he replied. "I do not know myself in those English phrases. I am an old Savoyard, an old Franciscan—that is me. I am an old *curé de campagne*. Let us warm ourselves and relax a little. That is what I like, for I am a lazy old rascal."

Father Ellis almost smiled.

"That is what I envy in my Gallic brethren," he said. "They know how to relax."

"Well, and why not?" said Father Happé. "We are not the good God—we do not have to keep the sun, the moon and the stars in their places! Thee world will not come to an end if we stop thinking about it for an hour!"

He noticed that Father Ellis was staring at him.

"It is most peculiar that you should say that," said the dingy little priest slowly. "I came today...that is...well, perhaps I had better explain. I wished to go to confession, but also to get a little direction...perhaps if I may tell you, Father..."

"*Dites, mon brave,*" said the old kind voice of Father Happé.

And, so encouraged, slowly and complicatedly and with great diffidence, Father James Ellis told his story; which may be reduced to the following facts.

He was the only priest in a mushroom manufacturing village in Essex—really no better than a suburb of the East End—a place whence you could see nothing but flat miles of factory buildings and jerry-built houses for the factory workers and cheap shops in which the workers bought the tinned food, frozen meat, and artificially whitened bread on which they lived. In the presbytery, whose walls were of little better than cardboard, there lived with him his mother and his sister—ostensibly to keep house for him, but actually because they had nowhere else to live and not a penny to live on. His salary was one on which three peasants could have lived in Savoy, but on which it was not possible for three people to live in that suburb, if they insisted on respectability, without slow starvation. And having starved slowly for two years, living on tea, bread and margarine and tobacco, the latter of the vilest quality and smallest imaginable quantity, Father James Ellis did not feel in himself the physical strength to go on watching his mother and sister starve and at the same time to say Mass every morning, preach twice on Sundays, hear confessions and visit his congregation.

"It is giving scandal," he said in the vague tones of the completely exhausted, "because I never give a copper to beggars who come to my door."

And then, still vaguely, but with a note of desperation which only comes into the speech of very good people into whose mind complaint never enters until injustice has done everything, Father James Ellis told the old Franciscan that he was afraid of saying Mass because he found in himself constant rebellion against God. "I fight against God," said Father Ellis.

It was then that the Guardian and Father Hilary happened to come out of the Guardian's room and to pass Father Happé's door. Father Ellis's tones would have been too low for them to notice, but there was a ring in Father Happé's answer that carried his words clearly to them:

"My dear Father, *mon brave ami*," said Father Happé, "I am there with you. I am one who fights God, and accuses God. Nobody knows it, but it is true."

"What…what, Father?" stammered his visitor after a moment in which the Guardian and Father Hilary had stiffened, hesitated, and had gone on their way trying to insist to themselves that they could not have heard what they thought they had heard.

"I accuse God of having forsaken me," said Father Happé. "Seeing the evil and injustice of the world, my soul dies a mystical death upon that cross, and I do not fear to cry what my Christ cried: 'My God, my God, why hast Thou forsaken me?' Be sure, *mon père, mon cher ami*, that is not the quoting of Holy Scripture merely! I say then to Him: 'I will not let Thee go unless Thou bless me!' I fight Him. And I fight on and on!"

From a priest's tears, the angels must hide their faces, for in his sorrow his likeness to Christ is revealed. A narrative must break off there. If any would watch with him, their place is "a little farther off" from the cavern of the winepress which he treads alone.

Glancing at Father Happé during Vespers, the Guardian found he had nothing to say to him about the words he had overheard, for Father Happé was wholly absorbed in standing beside the cross of his friend.

His only comment was to say, next morning when the Great Silence ended in the friary: "Oh, Father Savinius, I said Mass for your intention this morning,"—a gruff statement which made the Savoyard look after him in gratitude which made him forget to speak his thanks.

The *Daily Flash* continued the narrative in headlines and blurred photographs. "Roman Catholic Priest's Mother Dies Beside Gas Oven" it said on the hoardings, being rather short of news, and hinting as well as it dared at the suicide which was better news value than sudden death. The deceased, it said, had been found by her son on his return from church, where he had been delayed. The gas of the oven had been turned on but not lit, and she was lying with her head close to the open oven door.

A scrawled envelope brought the full story to Father Savinius.

"Dear Reverend Father," it said on the paper out of the twopenny packet. "You will have seen the newspapers, and will, I believe have remembered my dear mother in your holy Mass. The facts are as follows. I did not return home by the usual time that morning as I had been fetched to a sick call. My sister was away for a few days, visiting an old school friend. My dear mother had been preparing a little breakfast dish, and finding I did not return, had evidently decided to keep it warm in the oven; but with her thoughts always for me and never for herself, she had not had her own cup of tea, and evidently fell in a dead faint, possibly turning on the tap with her arm as she fell, but the exact explanation we shall never know. The police have been very kind, but her emaciated condition made them a little uncertain (none happened to be Catholics) as to whether she had not taken her life. However, they were soon satisfied that such an act would have been of the highest improbability in this case, and so it is all over. Everyone has been most sympathetic. It was her wish to be buried in her wedding dress, and when my sister went to find this treasure, she came upon a great many old letters, among them no less than two hundred written by my grandmother to her betrothed when she was in the Cape of Good Hope. She was showing these to the doctor, when he remarked that certain of the triangular Cape stamps were worth money. He was good enough to take away the envelopes, and to our great astonishment these are to be sold by auction by a most reputable firm. He says we may hope they will cover the cost of the funeral."

The letter continued on spiritual matters.

A fortnight later, Father Happé was on his way to lecture to the Royal Geological Society when, about to cross Victoria Street, he was pulled back on to the pavement (and incidentally from under the bonnet of a motor lorry which he had not noticed) by the bony hand of Father James Ellis.

"You must spare me ten minutes," said Father Ellis, when Father Happé had retrieved his hat and had finished nodding amiably at the driver of the van whose language consisted of words mercifully not in his English vocabulary.

He found himself ordered to eat a lifeless handful of dough pitted with dried raisins and spice which he knew was called a bun, and to drink something like a decoction of dead mice which was known as coffee. And thus fortified, he received Father James Ellis' news.

"Two thousand pounds! They weren't after all, the best kind of triangular Cape, but they fetched two thousand pounds!"

Evidently, to Father Ellis, this was millions out of the moon.

"What do you think now?" asked Father Happé, dropping his quite priceless treatise—of which he had kept no copy—on the floor, in his furtive endeavour to get the teashop cat to help him with his unspeakable bun.

"I can't think at all," said Father Ellis. "Fancy them lying there all those years. Any time in the last twenty years they would have been worth as much."

"But not so much as those years," said Father Happé. He looked disappointedly after the cat. "But as long as you don't try to think all will go well. Do not forget that we cannot understand."

"No," was the response. "I cannot understand why she should have had to die before we could find them. Any day she could have told us she had those letters. And then she would be alive to share our little comforts."

"You think she lacks little comforts with the eternal God?"

"No, no, of course not, my dear Father, but…"

"Her share of the treasure," said Father Happé, "was that death so soon after Holy Communion, a death in the act of doing a loving kindness for her son. She was old. It was most…sweet."

For the rest, Father Ellis found him absent-minded, but he had the satisfaction of having been able to give him a nice cup of coffee and a bun, which filled his utterly generous soul—so long starved of giving—with praise of God.

They had parted—and Father Happé was in the vestibule of the august society, attended by a respectful secretary, before he came to his own conclusion on the subject, muttering audibly: "The answer was not the answer. The agony itself was the answer. Such a little man to be allowed so much."

Chapter VI

The Screen Value of Father Happé

THERE WAS ANOTHER INCIDENT of which Shingle Bay never heard. It began on the backstairs of Trumpington Towers when Father Happé, returning from the room of the kitchen maid who was dangerously ill with pneumonia, opened the wrong door before the housekeeper could stop him, and precipitated himself into the dressing room of Sir Alberic Vaughn-Griffeths.

"What the...!" began Sir Alberic, who was at that instant having the worst of a wrestling match with his evening tie. His scowl would have killed anyone less resilient than Father Happé before his next words could have prevented it. "Bless my soul, if it isn't Professor Happé!"

And explanations and exclamations filled the air until Sir Alberic summed up the situation by saying:

"I shall tell Isabel to telephone, and if necessary I shall keep you here by pullin' up the drawbridge—though that hasn't bin done for a few hundred years, eh?—because I am convinced you are totally wrong about the Manila fossil and I'm goin' to get you into my laboratory and prove it!"

Father Happé, under his title of Professor Happé, was taken downstairs arm in arm, and introduced to Lady Vaughn-Griffeths, who could not quite understand how he had come to be in the attic, and looked as though she thought he had fallen out of the moon. She went amiably to the telephone and came back with the Guardian's permission for him to stay the night, so as to give Sir Alberic every opportunity of proving him totally wrong about the Manila fossil.

The household did not consist solely of Sir Alberic and his wife, as the noise from the small drawing-room proved. Father Happé was suddenly ushered—certainly with apologies, but as he was thinking of the fossil he did not hear them—into the midst of a wild herd of house-party. "My daughter's friends, who came to celebrate her birthday yesterday."

What he saw was a large and jostling throng of boyish-looking girls and girlish-looking boys, drinking something blue out of small glasses.

If the noise underwent a lull at his entrance, it was merely because the company were struck dumb at and by his appearance.

Sir Alberic introduced him by means of introducing them:

"These lunatics, Professor, are my daughter's friends. Chantal, you are honoured by the presence of the greatest geologist I have ever met."

Father Happé blinked.

"I hope," he said mildly, "if I ask for one of zoze biscuits, you will not fell it necessary to give me a stone."

The company were glad to have an excuse to shout with laughter, and in a moment Father Happé was the centre of a friendly mob, of which the foremost, a very pretty girl, offered him a dose of the blue mixture.

"We will drink your health in my new cocktail," she said. "It is called 'Gentians.'"

"Well," said Father Happé, eyeing the glass with curiosity, "That is very charming, because I am a Savoyard, and I was born among the gentians, but I feel like Socrates, when he was given the hemlock. I think it is poison." However, as one to whom death was no matter, he drank it at one draught, and did not cough.

"Good lord," said one of the young men, "you must have a throat, sir."

Father Happé surveyed him with charity.

"I was used," he said, "to drinking real drinks."

From that moment he could only be described, as he was most vociferously described, as "a riot."

It is no good wondering how he salved his permission to stay on geological business with the fact that, at 11 p.m., he was still surrounded by that most ungeological mob, because he had long ago forgotten anything but the mob. He was talking to them about drama and the screen. Even Sir Alberic and Lady Isabel were listening.

"I remember," he was saying, "something my friend Ramon y Cruz once told me..."

There he was interrupted by twenty voices, for Ramon y Cruz had been, first of all a film star of the first magnitude, and secondly a person of the most unsavoury reputation.

"Yes, yes, he was my friend," said Father Happé, bewildered. "I met him in the train going to Fribourg. He was my friend for many years—until he died. I was with him when he died. It was then he told me this. He said to me that, in drama, when everyone is watching the window by which the villain shall come, suddenly, he has come by the door!..."

Father Happé, absorbed in this visualisation, telling it with his hands and his whole being, made his whole audience watch him.

"We are looking at the window there!" he said, pointing slowly to where the heavy grey velvet swung from ceiling to floor.

Then he turned as though against his will:

"And the real happening is standing...there!"

As his gesture seemed to make the drawing-room door the one focus of the room, it opened noiselessly. One of the girls drew in her breath like a scream. For a motionless figure did stand there.

"If you please my lady..."

"Yes, Wilking, what is it?" said Lady Vaughn-Griffeths, with the impatience of a dignified individual who has been startled.

"Pardon, my lady, I thought I should...Father Happé, my lady."

"Well, what about Father Happé?"

Wilkins was new to his post, and easily rattled.

"She is dead, my lady," he blurted out.

Father Happé was across the room in a kind of effortless quickness. They heard his running upstairs.

When he came back, half an hour later, it was to a subdued party, who made way for him, and questioned him as soon as was decent.

"It was a collapse," he said tranquilly, sitting down in the chair they offered him by the big log-fire. "She was quite all right. She had received the Last Sacraments this evening."

"Eugh!" shivered one of the girls, who looked as though she had shed tears of nervousness. "Just when you were saying that."

"What is stranger," said Father Happé, peacefully, "is that what Ramon said—he was speaking Spanish and it does not sound the same in English—is that Death stood in the door."

They seemed to change into a bunch of children as he looked at them. Pagan children, who knew they would have to go out into the dark. He had compassion on them, and was wondering what to do for them, when one of the young men said—also with good intent to turn their thoughts from fear:

"You know, Padre, you were wizard when you pointed to the window and then to the door! Didn't Ramon ever tell you you had screen value?"

Father Happé laughed.

"Oh, yes," he said, "I always promised him to go on the screen if I found, after all, that I had time to spare! He promised me a great, great amount of money! Ah, my Ramon, he had more than screen value! He made great mistakes and everyone heard about those, but few people heard about when he changed his mind. He became one of the bravest men I have ever known. He left me forty thousand pounds to spend for the poor, and he said, though he could hardly speak for pain, but he loved to joke: 'Buy them everything that has no screen value.'"

Wilkins was new to his
post and easily rattled—
"She's dead, my lady"
he blurted out. —

As he said it, he felt them afraid, as he could have felt the fear that passes over animals in the mountains at presage of an avalanche. He looked up at them, and read that they knew in themselves they had nothing, save that which was of that celluloid currency. His hostess tried to talk about going to bed—a point on which Sir Alberic entirely agreed, but in the end Father Happé was made to stay on a little with the young people.

Turning to the first distraction that entered his mind, he sat down at the piano.

"Sit down by the fire," he said, "drink a little and smoke; for you have been startled. I should not have talked so. It is not death that you should expect, but God Who made you. There is a piece in the Psalms: 'Expect the Lord, do manfully, and comfort thy heart'—there is nothing else to expect, and God knows nothing worse than the truth about us, which is very comfortable when someone knows that. Now I shall play to you and you shall be comfortable a little."

They obeyed him, somehow, handing cigarettes and shaking some more cocktails; but before many minutes were over, they were only listening. For Père Happé forgot them, and played nothing but his bliss that the little kitchenmaid had confessed her sins and had received her Redeemer, and had gone to Him. He improvised, revelling in the glorious grand piano, the like of which he had not touched for many years. His music had the force of Stravinsky, the melody of Ravel, the capacity of Mussorsky. It was great, glorious, crashing stuff, tremendous with an overwhelming gentleness. And his fingers found it all, and one or two of his listeners, students of music themselves, could find no flaw of technique.

At last, beg as they might, he could play no more. He stopped, getting his breath, and pulling an old red handkerchief from his pocket, wiped his forehead, smiling with glory.

"Aië!" he said, "I did not think I should play again like that! One never knows what awaits one! One never knows!"

The others, watching him and loving him for his happiness, as human beings love those whom they see in that legendary state, understood why happiness was possible to him.

He did not sleep at all that night. He sat up talking with three of the young men until dawn, and then they motored him back to the monastery and heard his Mass.

Chapter VII

The Utter Undoing of Father Happé

RS. GARDEN, AS HAS BEEN SAID earlier in this narrative, had plenty of children. She urged this fact as an argument that Father Happé should spend his summer holidays with them at Hollyberry Farm, Ledbury, and Father Happé accepted it as an undeniable argument. Because when he was with children, he was at peace with the world. But then he had not met Leonora. Leonora was six. She was the youngest Garden but three. He had not met her because she spent most of her time with her grandmother, who was a silent old lady on whom Leonora doted. She did not come to the station to meet hi, and when he came back, vociferously escorted by Joe, Christine, Martin, and even small Sam, she was not even at the gate with her mother. Nor was she at tea. She had elected to have tea with the farmer and his wife. So Father Happé had entirely forgotten that she existed when, strolling alone in the little meadow that sloped down between the farmhouse and the road, easy in an alpaca jacket, puffing his pipe, a voice came out of the ground and said:

"Git off the grass!"

Father Happé leapt in the air, and gruff laughter pealed forth.

Peering down and about him, Father Happé saw a battered canvas shoe of very small dimensions abutting on the tiny path from which he, absentmindedly, had strayed. And pushing aside the tall hay-grass, he saw Leonora sitting in a rabbit-warren. She had judicial brown eyes, close-cropped fine hair to match, an oval face, a cotton smock once honey-coloured and now stained with the red soil. She was the smallest six-year-old he had ever seen. On her head was an old hat that obviously had belonged to the farmer. It had been made to fit with the help of crumpled newspaper. And it had been trimmed with long feathers of red sorrel.

"Oh," said Leonora. "I thought your legs were Mr. Billing's legs."

"Who," said Father Happé, "is Mr. Billing?"

"The cow-man," said Leonora. "I love him. He has a lovely smell."

"I am sorry," said Father Happé, "that I am not Mr. Billing." Under the gaze of those brown eyes in the very small face, for the first time in his life he felt slightly at a loss.

"Why," said Leonora, staring unfeignedly, "do you talk like that?"

Father Happé pulled himself together by instincts of self-preservation and self-assertion.

"Because," he said, sitting down beside Leonora, but not alarmingly near, "I have a language of my own, and I cannot speak any other very well."

Leonora beamed all over her face.

"An' I have that," she said firmly. "A langwidge. An' I can't. But sometimes I *can*," she added, as she wished to continue the cross-examination and foresaw difficulties. "I can..." she pursued, "when I have my hat on."

"It is a most splendid hat," was the reply.

Leonora accepted the compliment carelessly. She watched the visitor draw unavailingly at his pipe, and finally shake out the dottel of tobacco.

"Do that again," she commanded. "Put it in an' do it with a match. And then turn it upside down."

"But it would fall out!" objected Father Happé, obeying the first part of her instruction.

"Mr. Billing's doesn't," said Leonora triumphantly, and seated herself more firmly in her rabbit hole (and, presumably, in her devotion to Mr. Billing). She took off her hat and admired it, and forgetting the linguistic difficulties inherent in the act, by her own account, proceeded: "This is a very special hat."

"Do you wear it every day?" inquired Father Happé, as though he were a reporter collecting social gossip.

"Every day I wear it," said Leonora. "On Sundays I wear it for God." And she seemed to expect the conversation to proceed.

Father Happé sought a slightly more comfortable position on the bank which bordered the meadow. It was a steep little bank, and Leonora with her rabbit-hole had the advantage of him.

"You think," he said, his idiom making trouble for him, "that God likes you to do things for Him?"

Leonora regarded him with a gaze the clarity and severity of which excoriated his conscience.

"Don't you know," she said ponderously, "that that's a nintention? Don't you do nintentions? Sam does."

Father Happé knew that Jim and Myra Garden were the most Catholic parents possible, but remembering Sam, who was so small that while his excellent stomach and his jersey kept the front of his nether-garments in place, they slumped at the back, sometimes displaying an inch of his waistline in a very daring manner—remembering Sam (which was a distracting thing to begin to do) he felt he had underestimated Sam's asceticism.

"Oh, yes," he said, "I do...nintentions, too."

"What do you brush your teeth for?" demanded his inquisitor.

"Well," said Father Happé as soon as he could adjust his mind to it, "to keep them clean!"

Leonora rocked with laughter, squealing and jumping till her hat was disturbed.

"No," she said. "What do you do them for? I do mine that Mr. Billing may have a happy death."

But it would fall out!
objected Father Happé—

I am sorry to say that Father Happé's mouth opened and shut, and that at last he scratched his head. But fortunately this interested Miss Garden.

"It's a midge," she said. "I have got bumps almost everywhere." She scratched her ankles with the air of one rediscovering a pastime. "Shall we go down to the little shop and buy some pear-drops?"

Father Happé, looking at the face inclined interrogatively towards him, felt glad that he was on holiday and had some coppers and even a sixpence or two in his pocket.

"Yes, we shall," he said, getting to his feet.

"And a nice?"

"A nice what?"

Leonora was so entranced with her new comedian, that she took his hand while jumping with amusement.

"A nice in a cornet of *corse!*"

This was beyond Father Happé. As a novice out for a walk with his Superior, he kept a respectful silence, and listened to a conversation partially unintelligible, largely because it was an account of the doings of people of whom he had never heard but whom he presumed to be local magnates like Mr. Billing. His trained observation and his intelligence helped him to identify the "cornet," when in the small shop that smelt of chaff and bacon and paraffin. Mrs. Betsey Higman, Licensed to Sell Tobacco, pressed a primrose-coloured substance into something like a clown's hat made out of wafer-bisuit. In answer to her inquiry and Leonora's urging, he agreed to have one too; and they both emerged licking in unison, Leonora having demonstrated the technique.

He even agreed to keep a pear-drop in the corner of his mouth while doing so, "because it tasted funny." But, amateur where his mentor was professional, he choked. And when he had got his breath and wiped his eyes, he was distressed to see Leonora very pale. He made some cheerful remark, and tried to take her hand, but she drew away, and walked behind him. It is very difficult to carry on a tranquil social conversation with somebody who walks behind you, especially when that person is so small. For once, Father Happé was glad about his own lack of inches so that the difference was not greater. There is no saying how long this estrangement might not have continued, and for how long Father Happé might not have been ostracised for the unpardonable solecism of having been unable to breathe, had not a goat appeared from nowhere and stood like Apollyon in the way, regarding them with its pebble-pale eyes.

Leonora drew very close to Father Happé, and Father Happé felt suddenly pleased, because there was nothing he did not know about goats—knowledge half a century old and learnt on the slopes of the Alps, but applicable to an English goat. His gestures and his expressions were so well understood, that in a moment Leonora was smiling, albeit rather palely, at the departure of the menace.

"Was that your langwidge?" she wanted to know.

"Yes," said Father Happé.

"It's a good langwidge, isn't it? Ju think Mr. Billing has got a langwidge?"

Father Happé thought Mr. Billing probably had, but unless it can be decided charitably that he judged languages of Mr. Billing's kind unworthy of the Church's recognition, one is bound to be distressed by his reply.

"No," he said.

Miss Garden finished her "cornet" with a certain abandon, and turned to the pennyworth of pear-drops. With her mouth full, she became meditative, and after surveying Father Happé's stature and considering his beard, inquired:

"How late may you stay up?"

"All night if I want to," said Father Happé.

"Oh," said Leonora, and added without much hope of impressing him—the multimillionaire of late hours, "I can stay up till seven."

"It is getting late, now," said Father Happé. "The sun's gone over the hill, and the moths are flying," he added, as one blundered by.

"I don't like moths. You tell me about…when you were a little boy."

For the first time in his life, Father Happé *showed off*. He told of his prowess with a fierce pig, of how he found the eggs of the little black hen, though the whole household could not discover where she nested, and of how, when he was not much older than Leonora, he had climbed on the roofs of cottages—Leonora did not know how near those roofs had been to the mountain-side—and had shouted down the chimneys to startle inhabitants.

This last feat filled the heart of Leonora with the uttermost beatitude. She sighed, and skipped beside him, caring nothing for moths. Mr. Billing was deposed. What was it to slap the cows on their bony rumps compared with shouting down the chimney?

"And now," said Father Happé, as they came into the yard of the farm, "let us find your mother."

"It's not seven."

"No, but it is getting late. And what about supper?"

"Will you come and see me when I am in bed? Will…will you play boats in my soup?…An' I'll say all the prayers I know."

"Oh, there you are!" said Mrs. Garden, appearing with Sam by the hand and the baby, Matthew, under the other arm. "Jim's been looking everywhere for you. There's a telephone message from your publishers about the German edition of your last book. Jim's got it written down." She tried not to smile at the pair, because, what with Leonora's hat and Father Happé's rotundity, they looked so extremely odd. "Leo, my love, your soup is on the table."

"We are going to play boats in it," said Leonora, leading the way.

Boats were played; and with only a brief parting necessitated by bathtime, the evening's entertainment was continued under the eaves of the whitewashed attic, where Leonora, looking meek and melting to the heart, sat up alone in the bed she would later share with her elder sister, and recited not very accurate versions of the

Salve Regina and the *Creed*. She then, while Father Happé sat in attendance as though she had been a Bishop, invoked the protection of heaven on her parents and Mr. Billing and the cows and Mr. Billing's mother and the hens and all kind friends. "And make me grow up very soon," she continued, her eyes screwed more tightly than before, "and shout down the chimbley and be a nun, amen."

"And now," she said, wriggling under the coverings, "you say some of your langwidge."

For a full two minutes, Father Happé, obedient as a great tenor at a command performance, recited the magic lines of Leconte de Lisle:

"Couronnés de thym et de marjolaine
Les Elfes joyeux dansent sur la plain..."

And then his most elfin audience, who had been named for so great a Pope, was as deeply asleep as the flowers in the meadow below.

Jim Garden came up to fetch his guest down to supper, and he found Father Happé sitting beside the bed, regarding the tiny face turned to the pillow and the hands relaxing, the fingers uncurling to leave the palm spread to the bounty of dreams.

"She's a piece, if there ever was one," he said, looking down at her.

Father Happé shook his head. "She is Eve and the Holy Innocents in one," he said. "In an hour, two hours with her, I find I have still vanity and jealousy. She mocked me because I had not the talents of the cowman, and I displayed all my cleverness like a peacock. So she has humbled me that way, but she has done more. I did not know until I walked with her how very small one has to be 'to become like a little child.' I thought I was a little small man, but I was much too big to walk with her."

CHAPTER VIII

The Hiking of Father Happé

IT WAS A LOVELY SUMMER DAY, and the view from Reigate Hill is one of the furthest in England, so the three people sitting on its heights were well content. They were all dressed alike in brown corduroy shorts and brown cotton shirts and brown berets, and reading from left to right they were Ethel and Tom Barnett and Ethel's friend, May Turner. They were eating sandwiches of doughy bread and tinned salmon, washed down by mineral water, and they looked remarkably well on it. They were members of the Streatham Smashers, one of the most enthusiastic hiking clubs in the country.

"All right, this?" said Tom, gazing at the view.

"Suits me," said May, wrinkling her nose in the sunshine as if to let it know she appreciated it.

"'M," said Ethel—who, it must be admitted, took rather large mouthfuls.

But at that moment, there bowled past them, down the steep and slippery turf unhindered by a long rope of bramble which did its best to stop the wild descent, the body of the shortest and roundest man imaginable, clad in rusty black. Before him bowled his rusty black hat. And, languidly, the bramble tore a strip of cloth from one knee as it passed.

Tom was on his feet, had leapt forward, and flung himself at the disappearing body in a Rugby tackle. They disappeared into a clump of bushes which crashed around them. But Tom had effected a rescue, and he reappeared, scratched in the face and breathless, helping the little man, who was like an apple-cheeked, bearded, Humpty Dumpty. If the rescued party was lacking in gratitude it was because he was entirely lacking in breath. It was evident that he was a clergyman.

Much concerned, and all the kinder because they were stifling so strong a desire to giggle and feared he would notice it, Ethel and May made room for him beside them, and Ethel poured him out some ginger-beer. When he could hold the cup steady, and had enough breath to last him for a moment while he drank, the rotund person drank. But only for a moment. He put the cup down and peered into it.

"Good God," he said as though he were praying, "what ees it? You ought not to drink that."

Not being accustomed to spherical clergymen who invoked the Deity about ginger-beer unless they were "asking a blessing" on it, which this one certainly wasn't, Ethel and May—and Tom too, for that matter—were more than a little shocked. Their religious upbringing had been somewhat vague (Ma liked to go to church in the evening somewhere, but Pa didn't believe in anything) but they held to the tradition that clergymen ought to behave nicely. Tom said—unable to think of anything else to say:

"Well, what is it we had ought to drink?"

"Wine," said the clergyman, mopping his head. "Wine is the natural drink of the 'uman race. But in England, most of the wine is made from dried grapes, some water, and some wood-alcohol (he pronounced it *alcool*, which added to the mystery). That is not wine—it is stomach-rotter. But what this is you have so kindly given me, I do not know."

"You're not English, then," said Tom, solving the whole problem. For foreign clergymen to trundle, head first, downhill, and swear and tell people to drink wine was probably normal. And it was interesting to meet one.

"I am a Savoyard…where the cabbages come from," said Father Happé, trotting out the little joke that always went down well at Shingle Bay.

By luck, Tom knew where Savoy was—having seen it on a map in the office.

"Oh, there!" he said. "Well, you speak very good English, considering!"

He got up and saved some papers that had fallen out of Father Happé's pocket, and were now fluttering in a gorse-bush. Among them was an envelope, addressed to "Father Savinius Happé," to which name a great number of impressive looking letters were added. And another letter was addressed in spidery writing under a foreign stamp, to "Professor Happé." Tom was glad of the warning. The matter was explained even further. The clergyman was not only foreign, but a professor.

"Are these yours, sir?" he asked.

"Ah, yes. I am glad I did not lost those. Yes, I am Father Happé."

(Father Happy. Good thing he had not pronounced it Happ. Father Happy. Sounded like Father Christmas. Tom hoped the girls would not giggle.)

"Well," he said, doing the honours. "This is Miss May Turner, and this is my sister, Ethel, and my name's Barnett—Tom Barnett."

May marveled how the old man managed to bow while sitting down—and such a bow, too. She began to twiddle her hair and brush grass and dust off her shorts.

Ethel was puzzled. She had a friend who was "High" and who attended one or other of those churches in the City of London which had such strange old names—"St. Athanasius-against-the-Bishop," or "All-Martyrs-within-the-Wardrobe," but dashing and hail-fellow-well-met as was "Father" Bill Brummel, Rector of the latter, and "Father" Charlie Cranmer, Rector of the former, they resembled this little man as highly bred Bedlingtons resemble an old farm dog.

"Well, well," said Father Happé, whose senses were gradually returning, as his head ceased to be filled with blue catherine wheels and violet and orange rockets to the exclusion of all else, "I believe well that you have saved my life! Here am I—an old chap, isn't it, born and bred on the mountains, and I slip on what you call turf, and I could not save myself. Had I been barefoot I should not have slipped, you may be sure. You were so quick to have catched me."

"That's all right, sir," said Tom. "Live an outdoor life and your muscles will respond when you want them to."

"That is so right," said Father Happé, nodding vigorously, and then stopping because it set the catherine wheels in action again. "When I get home, I shall be so strong I shall scrub the floor and dig the garden and carry the coals, isn't it?"

These seemed curious occupations for a Professor or a High Church Rector.

"Are you going far?" May ventured.

"To Shingle Bay," said Father Happé.

"Walking!" exclaimed Ethel and May together.

"Yes," admitted Father Happé. "In such glorious weather, it is a pleasure."

"But it must be every bit of twenty miles, sir," said Tom, who saw the old man had no luggage. "You don't intend to do it before night."

"I shall try," said the old Savoyard. "If not, I shall sleep a while and then go on again. It will be a long time since I slept under the sky." He looked up at it as though it were an old friend with whom he had had many a feast.

"If you'll excuse me giving you advice, sir," said Tom, with the air of an expert, "I've done a bit of camping myself, but you won't try it without any equipment. The dew'll be heavy and you'll get chilled to the bone."

"Perhaps you're right," said Father Happé, accustomed to act on the suggestions of other people. "Then I must get on and begin this great walk."

"I wouldn't, sir. Break it in half. Stay the night somewhere."

Father Happé chuckled contentedly.

"No," he said. "I have no money for that. I had to give it to a poor woman who had had nothing to eat today, and had four little children."

Tom and Ethel exchanged glances. Did the old man not know the beggar's formula?

"Do you know the way?" Tom inquired.

"I shall ask," said Father Happé.

"Well," said Tom, "You let me put you on your road, sir. You keep up on the hills for another mile, and then take a narrow lane... Oh, come on Ethel, and you, May. Let's put... Father Happé on his road."

They got to their feet in instant agreement.

"But I cannot make you come my way," said Father Happé. "What is your way? Where are you going?"

"Oh, we aren't going anywhere," said Ethel cheerfully, "we're just hiking. I don't knokw where we're going. It's all the same to me."

Father Happé regarded her so pensively that she turned away shyly. She liked the old thing, though, my! he was queer to look at!

He said nothing until they had swung their haversacks on to their shoulders, and had climbed up the hill to where the old trackway showed in the turf. They made for it.

"That's your way, sir," said Tom. "We'll take you along there a bit. It's a very old road, but it gets there."

"Yes," said Father Happé. "It is perhaps six thousand years old."

"They call it the 'Pilgrims' Way' in these parts, don't they?" contributed Ethel.

"Ah yes, but that is a newer name. At first," said Father Happé, stopping to glance down at the vast plain shimmering in the heat between his vantage point and the line of the downs twenty miles ahead, "it was just the safe place to walk when all the plain was

forest in which there were wild animals. It was the highway between
the metal mines of Cornwall and Somerset and the east coast, too.
Probably men from Asia walked here and looked down on the
great fores. But, they were not pilgrims. They were merchants. It
was called the Pilgrims' Way when men walked here coming from
Glastonbury to Canterbury and Walsingham. And now," he said
meditatively, "it is the Hikers' Way."

The others laughed to show their appreciation of his ability to
make a joke in their language.

"No wonder," said Father Happé, "I had to stand on my head
to understand that."

Again they laughed; but he went on earnestly, trudging beside
them with a determined and yet easy step which they somehow knew
was the step of the mountaineer. "But how can you go nowhere?
When you come out of your front door, you must turn to right or
to left? Even if you get into the kind of aeroplane that goes straight
up, that is choosing your direction. No. You're not hikers. There
are no hikers. It is a story that there are hikers. You are pilgrims.
You go out to find something—though you do not know what
you shall find. You go out to do a great act of religion—to put a
poor man on his road. It is I that am much more the hiker. You see,
I am a Franciscan. And we have to go out into all the world and
live there, beckoned here and there, it does not matter very much
where, sometimes joining other Franciscans in a poor house that
is lent to us, but having no possessions. I have some books—a lot
of books that have been lent to me for my use. They are not mine.
When I get back, perhaps they may have been taken away. I have
only one thing—the whole world. Is that not enough? And am I
not a good hiker?"

They laughed again, but this time there was a certain affection
in the laughter: affection and respect and wonder.

"I thought Franciscan monks wore a grey sort of dress," said
Ethel.

"We cannot always wear our own uniform of poverty," said Father Happé. "We have to get someone to buy us these black clothes which make us look respectable."

"But don't you want to be respectable?" Ethel couldn't help demanding, being a young person who liked to get her facts right.

"It is a strange word," said Father Happé. "In my country we say a man is a good man or a bad man, a kind man or a hard man, a man who tried to save his poor soul, or a man who does not care to think where he is going, a man who does not care whether he does right or wrong. But here you say: 'He is very respectable.' 'You do not look respectable.' Bah! When God came on earth, did He tell everyone to be respectable? No. He said to Matthew, who was not always quite honest about tax-money, and James and John, who had great tempers, and Peter, who was unreliable, and Mary Magdalen, who was a bad woman: 'Follow Me!' 'Follow Me!' He said. 'They will persecute you and put you to your death, but follow Me!' And they did follow Him. And the pilgrims who made this way all bare on the grass, they were following Him. And I must follow Him. And you, so kind, coming out of your way to show me mine, you are following Him."

As May said afterwards, it wasn't as though he preached at you, but he seemed to be talking to himself, and you had to listen hard to make out what it was about, his language was so funny. He strode along on the ridgeway, the sun showing up the age of his black coat, and the sun shining on his head—he was holding his hat in one hand, and waving it when he was emphatic.

"But God looks after those who follow Him," he said. "He put you there on the hillside to catch me when I fell and to show me the right way. And to give me the pleasure of your company." He smiled jovially round, as though they were all boys together.

"Well, there *is* your road, sir," said Tom. "All you have got to do now is to go straight as an arrow straight due south. Straight home!" he added facetiously, half relieved and half sorry to part from his extraordinary acquaintance.

"No hiking now!" said Father Happé with many nods. "Ah, well, thank you infinitely. Good afternoon to you all. You are so kind." And with bows that were embarrassingly polite, he parted from them, diving down the lane, out of the sunshine.

"Walks as though he means to get there!" said Ethel.

Chapter IX

The Happiness of Father Happé

HE COTTAGE STOOD in a little clearing in the wood, among curious old lime-trees whose enormous boles had been split by the centuries, and whose leaves fluttered down on the autumn breeze. It was not a very old cottage. It had a roof, not a thatch, and its walls were—or had once been—painted white, but not half-timbered. Its garden had an old fence, painted perhaps at the same time as the walls, or very little later, and assisted by wire netting to keep out the rabbits. Though, to be sure, there was a rabbit inside at the moment when the story opens, sampling the extremely neat rows of vegetables which had been lately hoed, unlike the tangled flower beds where marigold and nasturtiums tangled their copper flowers.

It was very early in the morning. A robin, with the handle of a spade for a chanter's desk, sang his lauds.

And then the weather-beaten wooden door opened, and there came out a man so small and round, with grey hair and beard, dressed in a brown habit and a blue apron, that at the sight of him any unprejudiced beholder would instantly have believed in cobbolds or "good folk" or goblins or whatever you please to call them. The cobbold threw the robin a crust, sent a morsel of earth flying after the rabbit, inspected the vegetables, and went back indoors. He opened the door on the right, and taking off his apron, hung it on a nail. Then he went into the room on the left—a bare apartment whose walls were astonishingly frescoed, and which contained a single fine Persian rug spread before an oak chest, began to vest for Mass, with the assistance of a giant of a fellow who had just carried a legless man downstairs and set him in his wheel-chair with his Missal in his hands.

They called themselves the Giant, the Dwarf, and the Ogre. Their names were—in the same order—Oswald Walding, who looked the Viking his forebears had been, and who hammered at great lumps of stone because he was a sculptor, Father Savinius Happé, the authority on Etruscan civilisation, and Roger Campbell, who was a painter. It was Walding's cottage. But Roger Campbell lived there, and Walding carried him up and down stairs and was, as Roger said, a finer pair of legs to him than those he had left at Gallipoli. And Father Savinius Happé was there on holiday, recovering from an attack of measles, which ignominious complaint he had caught from a child in the village and which had gone hard with him. Thanks to the good sense of his superior, he was getting to look something like his old self. For not only was life in this cottage near to the life he had lived as a child in Savoy, but it permitted him to finish a book which he had been writing for ten years. Upstairs there were three rooms. Roger's, which faced north, as a painter's should—a cold apartment which was his heaven. Walding's, which faced west, and was a place of grey sheets and grey clay and chips of stone and dust of concrete. And a slip of a room which faced south and contained a chair and a table and piles of books which avalanched down into chaos now and then, making the dust rise and Father Happé sneeze.

Walding gave the orders and ran the errands. Roger gave advice. And Father Happé did the cooking and kept the kitchen clean. (It occurred to no one to clean the other rooms, though Walding made the beds and spread clean sheets on Saturdays, generally forgetting to wash his hands first.)

After Mass, came breakfast—bowls of coffee, black or white, and slices of bread with bacon between them. Then they would work till noon: then eat again, this time of bread and cheese and onions, washed down by beer or a harsh little Beaujolais. And then the house would fall silent until pangs of hunger rouse Roger or Walding—never Father Happé—to think of dinner, a grand affair, great platefuls of hot food, full of herbs and garlic. And after dinner, Roger sat in his chair between the open door and the stairs, looking out at the woods: Walding sat on the stairs, fiddle under chin: and Father Happé unaproned once more, sat at the piano on the landing —and played till he could play no longer. Then he finished his Office, gave the others his blessing, and they went to bed.

Sometimes they would all work in the garden. Sometimes they would talk the whole day through. Never, for one moment, in any department of their thoughts did any discord sound between them. Never was any one of them sad, though sometimes Walding had moods of silence, but these only ended in his getting up from a meal and beginning work without a by-your-leave. He had solved a problem: that was all. The others thought it no more worthy of remark than if he had blown his nose. A man's nose is his own; and so, in the philosophy of artists, are his thoughts.

Therefore, they noticed it when Roger fell silent in the middle of a meal, his silence having the quality of anxiety in it. And they were more at ease when he said: "This is Paradise. It is a life too good for our fallen nature. It can't last."

Walding shrugged his enormous shoulders. "You're like a woman, worried because she has nothing to worry about. Or like a dog who has killed his flea and is bored with nothing to scratch for." He turned to Father Happé. "What do you say, *mon père?*"

Father Happé scrunched an onion with a sound which would have made the refined shiver.

"I have been afraid myself," he admitted. "There is a peace in this house which makes me fear lest I should be unable to part from it. But that is nonsense of children. Peace is the food of the soul, and one goes from it stronger to fight."

"I have done my fighting," said Roger.

"If anyone wants to fight me," said Walding, cutting himself a lump of cheese as though he were hacking out a monument, "they can come and find me, and I shall throw sculpture out of the window at them. That's all the fighting I can manage. The good old primitive form of defence."

Father Happé got up, wiped his steel knife on his bread and ate the bread with its smear of butter, shook the crumbs off his habit, and with a gesture of his hand, as of one taking farewell of trifling matters, went back to work.

Walding pushed aside the cheese and helped himself to an apple. "Now, Roger," he said, "as I see it…" and embarked on matters relating to the *bas-relief* on which he was working. And Roger had no more moods. The expression of his thought had rid it of its power.

Late that evening they roused Father Happé from his books and sat in the garden while he cooked them a great dish of tripe, boiled potatoes, and cabbage. It was not as good as usual, and they found fault with it, venting their wrath on the Etruscans to whom he had given the attention that should have been given to the tripe. But it cannot have been badly cooked, because they went to bed after supper, and were asleep when the cottage door opened, and into the fantastic moonlight stepped Father Happé. The air was chill, but he had not put on his *capuchon*. He went down the road like a man going to keep a tryst.

He went, his hands in his sleeves and his head bent pensively, to a clearing in the woods where the blackberry sprays were full of fruit and there was an indescribable smell of autumn wild flowers—late honeysuckle and dusty hemlock. An owl looked at him, but Father Happé was unaware of this. He believed himself to be unobserved—or would have done, had he thought of himself at all. In the woods, he halted, and leaned against a pile of faggots which the woodcutter had left there, looking down where the chips showed white in the moonlight which was almost as clear as day.

Then he spoke aloud:

"Lord," he said, "the book is nearly done. If I were my own master I should add to it a monograph on the caves at Sutri. If I told Father Guardian I thought this necessary to the book, he would probably tell me to stay here until I had finished it. Till the spring. To be here through the winter. To see the snow in the woods, so like Savoy. You know, I am well once more. Perfectly strong. But another three months here would do me no harm, eh, Lord? I still have that slight deafness when I get overtired, don't I? I love this place. I love every branch of every tree I can see from my window. There is no nonsense in that little house, no lies, no criticism of one another, nothing but work and friendship. There is no hankering after fame or riches. Give them one good meal a day and they think they are living like lords. They think I am a master-cook, Lord, just because I rub their dishes with garlic! This is living at peace with one's neighbours as You meant one to live. They are good men, devoted to nothing but truth and beauty and friendship. Lord, let me stay in this Bethany! Lord, remember your friend Lazarus!" He was silent for a moment, and then he smiled all over his face. "No, I know. I only asked. Why not? I know. To create is Your privilege, which we share with you, we artists; but we must suffer with You if the likeness is to be complete. Lord, You are too good to me! There is no suffering in understanding this! It is like Palm Sunday—nothing but green branches. And the firs: their scent would absolve the world if it could! What can a man want in comparison with being made again in Your Likeness?"

The wind stirred among the trees, and a breeze rose, seeming to blow away the intense silence; but Father Happé fell silent, and stood still for a long while—so long, that the wild creatures began to reconnoitre round him. After a while he knelt down. He knelt so long that the business of the wood went on, at last, as though he had not been there. At last, his face, shadowed by his hood, turned up to the starlight.

For him the soft chill of the breeze was imperceptible. He did not smell the leaves. His eyes were shut to the starlight. He did not feel the damp, soaking his habit, nor the stiffness of his knees. He did not hear the owls and the rabbits cry, or hear the fox run down the path. A young lover is unconscious of his surroundings when he meets his beloved. Far more is a man unconscious of the pasteboard world around him when he perceives his contact with Reality, with the Greatest Personality, with the Lover and Creator.

Yet the Franciscan was not unmindful of the details of his own life. Before him, lying as though in the Lap of God, and shown to him by the Creating Hands, were the scenes of his life;—the Alps—his village lying beneath the conifers and juniper: then the sordid London streets to which he had been transplanted at the age of twelve, receiving a mental shock so great that it had perhaps retarded his growth; his entrance into a Franciscan school, then the novitiate; then—since it appeared impossible to teach him English and to make him of any use in the English Province, the sudden news that he was to be sent back to his own country—at least, next door to it, over the Alps to Fribourg. There, like a spring pent up, his nature had expanded and his mind had shown its abilities. University life had covered many years—in Fribourg, Padua, Paris, Rome. His Doctorate. The writing of books. And then the sudden order of the General which had sent him back to England—to Oxford. And so to Shingle Bay and parish life. He had been sent there, ostensibly to write his books in peace, but actually, he realised, to save his soul in humility after the years among the great scholars at the universities.

Father Happé smiled, and the moonlight played on his bent steel spectacles. From the height of his mind to the depths of it, he was thankful that he was a Franciscan, safe from the self-deluding of the man who has no Superior to see the truth about him. True, the Guardian did not understand much about the Etruscan civilisation, and often, Irishman as he was, had no notion of how an old

Savoyard philosophised. Nor did Father Hilary, the Englishman. But there was a mutual love, a mutual kindness…

He saw his life thus, lying in Those Hands.

"Lord," he said, "the world is in turmoil. Men have forgotten how to reason, and so they have forgotten to pray. Scholars are needed as never before. I would like to begin my life again, and teach philosophy. You know how long I have left. And you have put me in a little village."

Then he seemed to see, in the Hands, cherished as though they were birds sheltering there, the people with whom he had been brought into contact since he came to Shingle Bay—not only the parishioners but Alfred Webb, whom he had convinced of a better Communism (he was now under instruction by Father Hilary), Father James Ellis, the little kitchen-maid at Trumpington Towers and the young people at that cocktail party who had been frightened… Leonora, aged six, who had taught him a little humility, and those young hikers on the Pilgrims' Way…and so many more.

These were encounters of an infinite value. In their lives he had played a part to which he was bidden by eternal forces, and they had contributed to his life.

"Let me go back to the village…let me go on and do a little more," he begged, for beside what he had seen, his peace at the cottage and his prowess at the universities were nothing.

But ultimately even they were laid aside—these remembrances with the eternal light that explained them, and Father Happé was alone with God. In that aloneness, he saw that by the act of supreme lover, by which God in Himself is preferred before all else, a man does all that nature and grace together make him capable of doing—all that is necessary in the Plan of the Universe. In that act, all creation is blessed, all peace renewed.

Walding was up early next morning, but as he threw open the door, he saw Father Happé coming out of the woods with a bundle of sticks for kindling on his shoulder.

"Hullo, cobbold," he called. "You're up early! And you look well on it!"

"*All's* well!" returned the small brown figure, and it echoed through the trees like a shout of triumph. Then they went in to prepare for Mass.

Chapter X

The Loneliness of Father Happé

HEN FATHER HAPPÉ, his book completed, returned to the Friary at Shingle Bay, the Guardian met him at the door. "Ah, Father Savinius, welcome home!"

Father Savinius Happé grinned, waved the brown paper parcel containing his manuscript, and bowed to his Superior.

"It is done, Father Guardian, and I am done—done brown like your toast, isn't it?"

"Splendid! Splendid! Well, we're glad to have you back! And the great book is finished. Come in. I want five minutes with you before my taxi comes. I'm off to Birmingham."

"Not for long, I hope?"

"Cheer up, Father! You are going to have a really good Superior at last. I am being sent to Birmingham and Father Norbert is taking my place. He arrived last night."

Father Happé had been looking forward to showing his manuscript to his kind Superior. His face fell. But seeing Father Matthew's good spirits, he realised what a change it would be for him—moved from the tiny village to the big city parish.

"Ah," he said. "But that is excellent for you. All your energies will have so much to do, *hein?* We shall miss you so much. You have been so kind. But we shall be so glad to think of all the work you will make." (He meant "do.")

Father Matthew smiled, thinking that this would be a good phrase to repeat as his first joke on arrival at Birmingham.

"I must show my book to Father Hilary instead," went on the old Savoyard, cheering up, as he thought of Father Hilary's intelligent young face bent over the precious pages.

"No," said Father Matthew, after a moment's hesitation. "You must show it to the new Guardian, Father Norbert. Father Hilary is coming with me. He went on ahead yesterday—so sorry not to see you."

Father Happé sat down on the hard parlour chair, and put his brown paper parcel on the table.

"So!" he said, and nodded slowly.

There was a groaning rattle outside, as the Shingle Bay taxi drew up at the door. Father Happé stared out of the window at it. It had come to take Father Matthew away before he had time for a talk with him; and as for Father Hilary, he was gone.

"Come, Father," said a rather meticulous voice, and there was the thin figure of the new Guardian, watch in hand. "Ah, Father Savinius!" The smile was dutiful, but the cold eyes were vigilant. "When I saw you last you did not look so well. Quite ready to help a poor new Guardian?"

Father Savinius had bounced to his feet, achieved his foreign bow, which was his instinctive reaction of respect and obedience, and he nearly dazzled the new Guardian by his grin.

"Ready for anything, Father Guardian," he said. "Fit as a flea!" He was proud of the last simile—one of Walding's.

Father Norbert flinched. He did not like vulgarity. He did not like foreign manners. He did not like encountering great scholarship within the Order, and was fond of saying that simplicity was the mark of the true Franciscan, by which he meant the absence of anything remarkable. When the taxi had chugged down the drive he turned to Father Savinius with another polite smile.

"Come to my cell after Vespers," he said, "and tell me about your book. Father Matthew told me it was finished. So now you can help the community again."

With a nod, he went down the cloister, his quick neat steps like those of a well-trained school mistress.

Father Savinius went back to the ugly parlour, and picked up his parcel. It might have been a piece of knitting, as far as Father Norbert was concerned—a hobby on which no more time would be wasted. While if it had been Professor Voight, or the Marquis de la Tour S. Paul, or Mitchell of the British Museum, they would have forgotten their dinners to be allowed to look at the first chapter. He went up to his cell, which smelt of soft soap and the scrubbing brush, and threw the parcel into his cupboard. He changed into his habit, and went down to the chapel. In the sacristy he met Brother George, old and quiet.

"Ah, thank God you're back, Father," he said contentedly, like a man whose precious animals are safely folded. "You look well, indeed you do."

"I *am* well, Brother, and I thank God I *am* back," said Father Savinius, so happily and gently that the Brother looked after him as he went into chapel.

At recreation that night, Father Savinius saw what was before him for the winter. Spontaneity, which was the most attractive thing about the dozen young students, was chilled by the rather stilted manners of the new Guardian. Genteel, he had a way of seeming to notice every broadness of speech in the Yorkshire man and the Lancashire lad, every lack in table manners, every slightest tendency to slip on the smallest point of custom. To the nervous, he was curt. To the honest, repressive. And yet he was a good man, devoted to the interests of the Order and the community, careless of fatigue and of his strength, which was limited by constant neuritis. He was quite untainted by ambition, content to be buried at Shingle Bay for the winter and for as many years as his Provincial pleased. It was not his fault that he had been bred and born in an atmosphere where the accepted idea of order was that of a front parlour with all the mats in place.

Brother George
old and quiet.

"I want," he said that evening to Father Savinius, "I want you, my dear Father, to try to speak more correct English so that you will find your work in the confessional easier. I want you to take over the boys' club, and to be in charge of the farm and the Brothers. You will take Father Placid's place. I am changing everyone round, so as to put Father Henry in Father Hilary's place with the students."

He looked for a moment at the rotund figure before him, thinking how extraordinary it was that the Provincial should have suggested putting Father Savinius in Father Hilary's place. It was, of course, only a suggestion. Scholarship was not all, and what would this rough old countryman turn out if he were in charge of the students who were, already, far too rough?

Back in his cell, Father Savinius opened the window and listened thankfully to the soft sounds from the farm — sounds which only an ear accustomed to them would have traced. The gentle clink of a chain and sleepy sounds from the poultry. His gratitude to

Providence knew no bounds. For the first time in his life he was given an easy job. Father Norbert had the good reputation for not interfering with those placed in charge of this work or that; besides, Father Savinius knew that his Superior did not know a jot or tittle of the mysteries of farming and would ask nothing better than to leave them in the hands of one who was born to them.

So there began for Father Savinius a curiously solitary life. There was no longer in the community a single person to whom he could talk of intellectual matters. And, as the winter drew on, they forgot he was a famous scholar, and only thought of him as the old farmer whose queer ways were successful with animals. As for the stable cat, it worshipped him to such a point that the greatest ingenuity was required to keep it out of chapel, for it could not bear Father Savinius out of its sight, and would arrive, like a striped bombshell, from the choir windows if they were left open, to seek him, purring among the stalls. There had been the moment, blessed among the novices, when it had jumped on the Guardian's head. Had it not brought with a young rat, freshly killed, to witness to its attention to duty, its own death warrant would have been issued. But Father Norbert dreaded rats, and so it grew fat on its adoration, and had seven kittens on the Guardian's feast, a delicate Attention which the novices declared was a suggestion from Father Savinius.

Even the village seemed changed since his return. The Gardens had moved to a larger house a mile or two away. "Miss Cissy," now Mrs. George Allen, had gone to stay with her husband's people in Cornwall. Mr. Alfred Webb, late Communist, had found a job in London which would enable him to speak in Hyde Park for the Catholic Evidence Guild. Only one person, in all that long winter, came to talk to Father Savinius.

This was Lestrange who kept the Gift Shop. His wife had run away with the bank manager at Sandhampton. He was a lanky, saturnine fellow who looked clever and was far from it in practical matters, but possessed of a hungry brain and huge nervous hands which, given a bit of clay or a water-colour brush, would produce something delicate and vital. He came nominally to see Father Savinius about a boy in the Club who was clever with his fingers and whom he proposed to take on to help him with the fret-work tetapot stands and poker-work mottoes in which the Gift Shop did an excellent trade to visitors from Sandhampton who could find nothing else in the village to buy; but actually he came to confide his trouble.

"Yes," he said in the seclusion of the cowshed, where he was watching Father Savinius milking. "She's gone. I tell people she's away on a visit, but she's not coming back. We never hit it off. We had no children and when all her ideas about my becoming a famous artist ended in a shop at Shingle Bay, she had no further use for me. This chap Blandford's taken her to Paris and she thinks life's begun anew and all that. I haven't thought yet what'll have to be done. She won't come back. All I know is that if she came back tomorrow, it would make no difference to me, whatever it did to her immortal soul. Virtually, I've lived alone since we were married and I always shall. She has no more notion of what I'm thinking about than of the feelings of a black beetle. Odd thing is, I was always alone as a kid. Only child, brought up Protestant. Only turned Catholic when I was twenty. It's an odd life if you don't know what it's for and everybody you know thinks different. Isolates you. I bet," he added suddenly, pulling a straw from the manger and twisting it, "you're a bit isolated here with this lot of good Fathers?"

"Somtimes," said Father Savinius, his grizzled head against the red flank of Clover, "I would give all my meals and all my sleep for a day to talk with someone about the caves at Sutri."

"The *what*?"

"Oh," with a shrug and a shake of the head, "just some caves about which I ought to have written…about which I must write a monograph one day."

"I see. Your hobby. Like my bees. There isn't a da—, a single human being I ever meet who will talk bees with me. I dunno. I've got friends, of course, but they are married and live all over the place. It's not that I'm difficult, but I hate being bored and I hate boring people. And if ever I try to say what I really think to the people in this place, they look very suspiciously at me and appear to think I'm highbrow and trying to put it over them." His voice had the dreary anger of desperation.

He stared out across the cowshed, whose open door showed the playing field of the boys' club, where a few geese walked on the threadbare grass. A lay-brother, beside the clothes line that stretched between the fence and the bough of the wild plum tree, was taking down the long white strips, like winding sheets, that were altar cloths. The sea wind whipped them out as though they were pennants flying an invisible signal.

"Oh, go on, Father Savinius," he burst out, "talk religion. It's the only thing to talk. There's no other blasted thing to say."

"No," said Father Savinius, leaning against the chaff cutter. "There isn't. Not about loneliness. When I say my Mass in the early morning, when I set down my covered chalice and paten on that cold flat linen-covered altar, I feel: this is my soul, my mind and my feelings that I put here. I put them in the middle of my cold solitude and I offer them to God. God knows there is nothing else to do with them."

Guy Lestrange, like any other layman, was shocked at a priest saying what he would have said himself without a second thought.

"That sounds cynical, Father."

"Maybe," said the old Savoyard, picking up a kitten that clawed at his ankle, and tucking it in the crook of his arm to be stroked. "Truth often does. When we are left alone, we realise that there is nothing else for us but God, and that is what we have to realise sooner or later. But it is a taste of death to realise it. At death we shall have no distractions. We love our distractions, isn't it? You want a wife to love you and to talk about bees with you. I want to write my monograph. But God created me for Himself, not for the writing of this monograph. Loneliness is the price of individuality. The kittens are not lonely—only hungry or cold when they cry. It is the mind which is lonely, though the body has to feel it. My body misses the taste of the poor rough wine we drank at home and the herbs and the cheese and the garlic, for this English food tastes to me of plaster off the walls and that is all. But really it is my mind that knows that, and it is sad because in those days, the world was full of friends and those who loved me. We talked about our thoughts... My old uncle Jules was a great one for the talking of thoughts..."

"There was a girl I was in love with when I was young," said Guy Lestrange. "I suffered enough when she married someone else. But I'd give a lot to have someone to suffer about now."

"Loneliness," said Father Savinius, "is almost the last pain."

"The *last* being when you fail yourself," said Guy, and Father Savinius gave a nod, and put the kitten down to run to its mother.

"But meanwhile," said Father Savinius, picking up an empty pail, "you are alive, and not so very old, and the spring is coming. You may not think you are glad to be alive, but if you were hanging over a precipice from a tree that began to crack, you would make a fine struggle to save yourself."

"There is always tobacco," said Guy. "Have a fill?"

Father Savinius shook his head. "Thank you, I must get on with my work. Ah, well, we have consoled each other, isn't it?"

Guy growled. "A bit, because you didn't offer me any nonsense." He grinned, and for a moment they looked at each other and then at the same instant, laughed.

"You and your caves, Father!"

"You and your —— blasted bees!" returned Father Savinius, quoting exactly and affectionately.

It was a pity Father Norbert turned the corner of the cowshed at that moment. (But he always told himself that he must have imagined it, or that Father Savinius was using some technical word about bees which he did not know, or that, anyhow, Father Savinius's English was that little knowledge which is a dangerous thing.)

Chapter XI

The Failure of Father Happé

T'S FATHER SAVINIUS, Doctor," said the Guardian, rather fussily. "He's failing."

Dr. Deedle mentally called the new Guardian an old woman. Aloud, he suggested snappily:

"Well, let me see him. It won't help to talk about it." He was easily the rudest man in the county, but he was a Catholic and refused to charge the friary a penny, even when they had to call him out of his bed at night, and so, for twenty years, he had doctored them.

When the parlour door opened, and Father Savinius came in, Dr. Deedle forgot his irritation at first glance. The brown ball that was Father Savinius had shrunk. The bounce had gone out of it. The eyes behind the crooked glasses had lost their fire. Instantly Dr. Deedle assumed his armour of irritability.

"Well, well, Father Savinius, so you have been getting run down? Too much trouble, I suppose, to send for me and get a bottle of tonic. Have you been trying to fast?" (For Lent was half through.)

"No," said Father Savinius, with a little cluck, "I have been succeeding! It is no trouble to me to fast. I do not want to eat. Your English food is not so attractive to a greedy old peasant."

"Any pain?"

"Yes. Quite a good lot of pain in my chest. But it is just pain—nothing remarkable."

"H'm." The more Dr. Deedle saw of Father Savinius, and the more he heard him say, the better he liked him; but he felt it would

Instantly Dr. Deedle assumed
his armour of irritability.

be unprofessional to let him have the slightest notion of this. "Well, I don't suppose you are much judge of your own health. Take off your habit. Let me have a look at you."

When Dr. Deedle drove away, Father Savinius was sitting beside him. Dr. Deedle thought he might as well take him to Sandhampton Hospital, as he was going there anyhow, and have an X-ray taken. On the journey, Dr. Deedle was very taciturn. Father Savinius was very quiet.

Arrived at the hospital, Father Happé (for he can have the name by which he was famous now that he is out of the friary) was asked to wait in a green-tiled room, furnished with some porcelain sinks and a few wooden chairs. He sat there obediently, and for a long time, because Sandhampton Hospital, being small and on a main road between two little towns, quite frequently has a number of casualties. They brought two into the little room where Father Happé waited: a man with his head tied up in stained, dirty handkerchiefs, who rolled it ceaselessly on his stretcher and groaned, and a burnt child, sobbing with terror. The Casualty Sister was a brisk, efficient young woman, quite unaffected by the sight of pain, as indeed she had to be to get her day's work done. She stood by, among the knot of distressed relations, while Dr. Deedle examined the man on the stretcher, and then gave orders to the orderlies, as though, thought Father Happé, she was telling them to remove a piece of furniture to the ward upstairs. She sat down beside the child, and, tucking the curly head under her arm, began to cut away blisters as if the shrieks had been Father Happé's imagination. Once, looking up, she caught his eye, and said: "It isn't hurting as much as it sounds. They always feel it their duty to scream," and gave him a surprisingly kind smile. When the screams were only sobs, as the bandaging was being done, she asked: "What are you here for?" And when he told her, looked at him shrewdly, and nodded.

"My God," said Father Happé to his Maker, "How can you create such women to be so undistressed? It is a good thing You do."

About an hour later, when he had grown very tired of his wooden chair, he was taken upstairs and handed over to a young nurse, who gave him a cup of tea and bade him undress and get into bed. It was a small ward, the medical ward. It was tiled half in blue and half in white, and decorated with a large photograph of the Countess of Sandhampton and four vases of daffodils arranged in a straight line on the centre table. There were twelve beds in it. In the corner next to his own, an old labourer was dying slowly by himself. He was unconscious, and gave no trouble. On the other side, a younger man was convalescent after pneumonia. The inmates of the beds who were well enough to stare stared at the short, odd little priest. They began a polite conversation among themselves about the weather and the crops, but finding that he took no part in it, allowed it to develop into a more cheerful one about Miss Madcap, who ought, by rights, to have won the three-thirty.

Father Happé, lying in his strange bed, twisted his rosary round his fingers and descended into hell. No one had ever called him an artist, and he had certainly never thought of himself as a peculiarly sensitive being, but for the first time in his life, since he had been a child of twelve looking out of a dirty window at the backs of south London houses and weeping for the Alps of Savoy, he told God he could not bear his environment. It was everything he loathed. It was impersonally kind: it was an institution: it was insensitive and smelt of antiseptic: it was without holiness of humanity. His soul seemed to vomit the realisation of it, refusing to bear it.

Father Happé lay still, his eyes shut, the agony of his mind making him entirely unconscious of the pain of his body, until the lights were out. Then, with the unconscious man on one side of him, and a snoring convalescent on the other, he turned on his face and wept into the shelter of his cold hands. From her cupboard-like room, with its door open into the ward, the night-sister could see the twelve beds. She saw and heard no disturbance from that end of the ward.

Father Happé was rebelling. He was fleeing from all that the hospital stood for, godless philanthropy without a trace of the supernatural to redeem it from its business of tidying up the towns of all trace of disease. He felt like a diseased thing thrown in this antiseptic bin. Oh to be standing in the steep street of his village… in the early morning…with a smudge of wood-smoke on his face, finishing his jobs for his mother before running down to serve Mass before the tawdry altar and the wonder-working statue of St. Anne! For one great breath of mountain air he would leave everything… everything. An hour there, climbing the paths slippery with pine-needles, smelling the snow, feeling the hot sun on bare legs and arms, and he would be well. He would live to be a hundred and five, like Great Uncle Pierre. God, that was human life, decent life, the life for Christians: not this place of abominable cleanness that had never been fresh!

Worn out, he fell asleep; and in his dream ran on, and on, down easy paths, leaping fallen trees, shouting to hear his voice ring and echo.

Suddenly he was awake. Sister was helping an orderly to wheel something out of the ward. The man in the next bed had stopped breathing. He had died like a dog, without a prayer. The body was being taken away.

He, a priest, had been in the next bed, and he had let that man die without absolution. He could have given him conditional absolution. But he had been dreaming of Savoy. "Could you not watch with Me one hour?" No. He had slept and dreamed—afraid of agony. And the man had died alone and unhelped.

"Awake, Father Happé?" said Sister in an efficient undertone. "Not comfortable?" She bent nearer and saw he had been weeping. She put her hand on his. "Why, you're in a nasty cold sweat. Is the pain so bad?"

"No, madame, thank you," said Father Happé. "I was just a little cold."

"Well, we'll soon get you warm," she said cheerfully, and was back in a minute or two with a steaming cup and a hot water bottle. "Now you'll feel ever so much better." She attended to him a little anxiously, because he had been simply a case who was to have an X-ray next day, and she had not thought twice about him. Now he had been drenched with sweat and there had been a look on his face…

"So he died," he said, sipping his hot milk.

"Yes, yes," said Sister. "A very happy release."

Father Happé sipped his milk. You might as well talk to an animal. What did she know of death, except the business of the body? Now if she had been a nun…

She took the empty cup, and tucked him up. And the hot water bottle in its regulation flannel cover, seemed to him the most human thing he had ever found in England. He took it into his bosom as though it had been a pigeon or a cat, and almost instantly fell asleep. What good was it to care? He had failed. He had wept and sweated. Mind and body could stand no more.

…

To find his hand lying in the hand of another person was so unusual that he sat up on his elbow. That brought him nearer to her, and he smelt something he could not identify. Not wood-smoke or pine-cones or incense or the freshness of wine, but like them all and yet not like them. It was an oval face, not young: tranquil, but with eyes of the deepest intentness, dark as the black columbine and with a mouth so expressive that without speech it seemed to be answering urgency. The hand that held his was supple, deft, perhaps hard palmed, perhaps rough, yet was it either? Was it not rather a hand used to a sceptre? Was it not so tender that the most restless child would not feel it in its sleep? He clutched it as though he were afraid of falling. "Who are you?"

"What is the matter, Francis Happé?"

"I let him die."

"Are you God?"

"I am a priest."

"What do you want?"

"Did he save his soul?"

"I was there."

"Why?"

A smile, magnificent, dark, luminous. "You wished it."

"I wished nothing."

"You are tired."

He realised they were talking the *patois* of his village. He tried to look at her dress, her shawl, her pelerine or whatever it was. It was so dark, dark purple, dark as to be almost black, like the glorious darkness when a hard light has been put out, shut out.

"I have a disease."

A nod, a light smile.

"No matter; but I want something to eat."

He was sitting up, and she was nearer. He had a great bunch of black grapes in his hands. He indicated them with a peasant jerk of his head, and asked the name of the vine. The answer came in the same fashion, naming the vineyard, talking of the soil, reminding him of the man who owned it: his son had it now; they had done well with their cows, and the younger son was married, too, and with two little girls. They were eating the grapes together. He told her how he and his cousin had gone to that vineyard one evening and been caught by the owner, who had dusted their jackets for them. Together they laughed. Then he said: "This disease. Will it be a long job? I don't think I can stand any more. I have failed, you know."

The reply was a smile, a smile into his eyes that warmed his being, a smile almost contemptuous as though to one who has made a trivial mistake out of carelessness. "You are very ignorant, Francis Happé," it said, with the omniscience of his own mother when he had hurt himself and was frightened by the blood. But now it was a great personal jest between them too, because she knew he was one of the greatest scholars in Europe. She knew the extent of his mind as she knew about his disease.

"I didn't mean to rebel," he told her. "I think I was worn out." He had never made an excuse for himself since he was a child, but it seemed natural to do so now. She assented, by a look in her eyes, so completely that the matter never crossed his mind again; instead, his thoughts leaped to her, set free. "I shall see Him!" She was grave with glory, like a bride. She drew her left hand from the darkness, and he saw it pierced close to the wrist by a long wound.

"His!"

"Flesh of my flesh."

He took it to his mouth like a cup, drinking at it with adoration. And the wound seemed to call to the pain that he had forgotten in his own body, and he heard her say: "Flesh of your flesh."

He looked up, to read in the marvellous eyes reiteration of the words which he understood yet dared not accept, and the hand under his grasping fingers grew, so that the fingers knew It before his eyes reached the Face and saw in one moment what Peter, John and Magdalen saw. He saw what the blindest tendency of the senses and the farthest flight of the intelligence of man look for.

"Master!"

...

"Were you awake early, Father Happé?" inquired the nurse, handing him his thick mug of tea and plate of undistinguished bread and butter.

"Yes, madame, very early. The birds woke me."

"That's a pity. Sister says you had a lot of pain in the night."

"I had a very good night. I am rested."

Next day, Dr. Deedle came and sat by his bed, and after some hum-ing and ha-ing and saying a rest would do him no harm, caught his eye, and became at once relived and snappish.

"That X-ray was not so good, yes?" suggested Father Happé contentedly.

"No," grunted Deedle.

"A big disease, *hein*?"

"...Yes. I'm sorry, Father Happé, but no good making a mystery of it to a man like you."

"You don't want to chop me into pieces, I hope?"

"No...I don't think that would do any good."

"That is fine."

"Of course, you had better have another opinion..."

"I have it," said Father Happé. "In myself. I know."

"Well, you're taking it in the right way," said Dr. Deedle, trying not to look at him.

Father Happé laughed.

Chapter XII

The Triumph of Father Happé

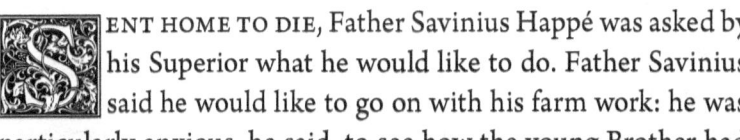ENT HOME TO DIE, Father Savinius Happé was asked by his Superior what he would like to do. Father Savinius said he would like to go on with his farm work: he was particularly anxious, he said, to see how the young Brother had managed while he was away in hospital for those few days. The new Guardian hesitated. He was just beginning to realise that when Father Savinius died there would be a good deal of fuss in the papers, because Father Savinius's book—which he had brought back from his stay in Oswald Walding's cottage done up in a brown paper parcel—was now reviewed in every serious newspaper and quarterly, and but for the fact that they believed Father Happé to be in Savoy, since he always spoke of himself as a Savoyard, the newspaper men would have been down on him like terriers on a hedgehog, standing round him and yapping questions.

But he had said Father Savinius might choose, and Father Savinius had chosen. Besides, he would be better out of doors, since the weather was mild, than sitting about indoors.

So Lent continued, and the primroses came out, and Father Savinius worked in the cowsheds, singing to himself the songs and hymns of his boyhood. One day there came into the cowshed Mrs. Garden and a small figure underneath a large hat—Leonora.

"We have come to see you, Father," said Myra Garden gently, "because we hear you have had a pain, and we are so sorry."

"In the tummy," said Leonora from under her hat.

"That is very kind of you," said Father Savinius, who was delighted with their visit, but anxious about their shoes. "But this is a very dirty cowshed."

"A lot of lovely smell," said Leonora. "'Smy birthday. I'm seven." She was such a very small seven.

"Then we must go and see the pigs," said Father savinius.

"In that case," said Leonora's mother, "I will go and see Father Guardian first, on business, and then perhaps when you have seen the pigs as much as you want to, I can talk to Father Savinius?"

The old man smiled at her.

"What is there to say but that it is a nice day and God is good?" he asked. "It is more important to see the pigs. Come, Leonora. There are two old pigs, and their names are Susanne and Casimir, and the young little pigs are Josephine and Aristide."

Leonora's grasp on his hand tightened. She found this highly satisfactory.

"What shall we give them?"

"Some milk and some potato skins," said Father Happé.

Leonora listened to their table-manners as to music, grinning all over her freckled face.

"Ju remember you came to Hollyberry Farm with us?" she asked, as though this event had happened in a previous incarnation. "And ju remember we got ices? I wish we had a nice now, don't you?"

Father Savinius shivered.

"No," he said. "It is not nearly warm enough."

Leonora giggled.

"You *are* funny!" she said. "Say some of your langwidge for me!"

Father Savinius struck an attitude, and thinking for the first time for years of Molière, harangued Leonora and the pigs in a speech from "Le Médicin malgré Lui." The pigs were only momentarily surprised, but Leonora was entranced, and stood on one leg, nibbling her thumb until Father Savinius could remember no more.

Leonora listened to
their table manners
as to music —

He modestly refused an encore, and suggested an inspection of the stable cat's second family of kittens.

In the dimness of the stable loft, sitting in the hay, her lap full of kittens, Leonora started a spiritual conversation.

"What do you think kittens know about God?"

"All they need."

"Oh. And what do you think the cat knows?"

"All she needs, too."

"Doesn't she think God very clever to let her have kittens? How do you think He thought of kittens?"

"I don't know."

"Don't you? You ought to know. Is there a lot you don't know?"

"Yes. An infinite lot that I do not know."

"Tell me what you do know."

It was with thanksgiving that Father Happé heard someone come into the stable. He looked down, and saw the Brother Sacristan.

"You want me, Brother?"

"Good gracious, Father Savinius, you shouldn't be climbing about! Can you come now, please? You know Father Mark was to be back from Trumpington to take Benediction? He's just telephoned to say he's had a puncture and can't be in time. Everyone's out, so will you come? They're expecting short Benediction, Stations and the sermon."

"We must go," said Father Savinius to Leonora. "I have to go to church."

"I'm coming to church because it's my seventh birthday," said Leonora. "But must we go yet?"

"I'm afraid we must."

"One always has to go," sighed Leonora.

"In heaven we can stay as long as we like to do anything," he told her.

There were not very many people in church, but there were the few who came because they liked to come, and one or two who came because they thought it right to come. Roger Campbell in his wheeled chair, "Miss Cissy" and her husband, back from Cornwall, Mrs. Badger, Mrs. Forbes-Chippenham, and a few more shopkeepers and villager.

They were surprised to see him, for the rumour had reached them that he was ill. He looked much thinner, but so vigorous and happy...

It was only as he began the Stations that the pain became more than he could manage. Still, nobody noticed anything, except that he spoke more slowly and a little less clearly. It was only when the Stations were ended, and he mounted the pulpit with something like hesitation, and then faced them, that they realised the rumour had not been untrue. The crooked spectacles slipped because his nose was thinner, and he put his hand up and took them off, and looked at them again without them. He looked much younger without them, and much more of a peasant.

It made everyone remember the first time he had come into a church to preach, and how they had gasped in astonishment at this short, stout man who appeared to be almost round, who had seemed to announce himself in his first words: "I am Happé"; when he had only been saying that he was happy to be with them for that great Feast of humility—Christmas.

"In the Name of the Father, and of the Son...and of the Holy Ghost," said Father Savinius. "My text is taken from...no, you must excuse me, please, that I do not give you the text, for I do not see very well. But it is the words spoken about the Apostles after the Transfiguration on Mount Thabor, when they had seen Moses and Elias, one on both sides of Our Lord. They had heard a voice from heaven saying: 'This is My Beloved Son,' and they had fallen to the ground, very much afraid. Then *'Jesus came and touched them, and said to them: Arise and fear not. And they, lifting up their eyes, saw no one, but only Jesus.'*"

He paused.

"You are going to die," he said. "All of you. You are condemned to death. Now that is a fine way to begin a sermon, you think! That is a cheerful way! But the truth is always cheerful, because it is safe. It is things that are not safe which frighten us—the wheel which may come off the cart, and the engine on the aeroplane which may not work. It is the thing that may perhaps happen which makes us anxious, not the thing which we are absolutely certain must happen. And death must happen. Now I know, my children, there is a way you like me to talk to you, and a way you do not like. You do not like, very much at all, the way I talk, because I talk English not well, and worst of all when I preach; and because I am an old peasant and you are ladies and gentlemen."

This was said with a politeness so naive and sincere that Roger Campbell writhed in his chair with satisfaction. God, God—*that*, said like that—now when they were just finding columns in their newspapers about the little man they had all made fun of, must be just puncturing their self-satisfaction where they would feel it most. And the old fellow was incapable of realising it.

"But listen to me for once, please. Because this is the one more sermon I shall preach. And I am going to do what I have always wanted to do: I am going to say to you what I want to say, most simply and with all my heart.

"My children, you would think it a great sin to disobey Our Lord about not believing what He says, but there is one thing He tells you, two things He tells you, that you do not do. How often did He say: 'Peace be with you'? And how often did He say: 'Fear not'? And yet I see you, good people who go to the sacraments, and so often you look as though you had no peace, and as though you were afraid of something. What are you afraid of? I know. You need not tell me. If you are a little child…" he was hesitating (the pain was winning) and looking down the church at Leonora, and at two little boys at the back… "you are afraid of things that grown up people do not understand. If you are…grown up, you are afraid of poverty, of being ill, of being out of work, of loneliness. I will not talk about those silly fears of what the people in the house nearby will think of you. I talk about real great fear.

"My children, I have been afraid. And God has sent to me some of those things that I was afraid of. But when one is afraid, greatly afraid, it is true that Jesus comes and touches the poor soul in its agony, and says to it... 'Get up from your fear: do not lie there in fear.' And the soul, if it looks up, will see no one but only Jesus. And will you be afraid of your Redeemer? He can do anything. He can come Himself to you, so that you are more sure that it is He than you are sure that your doctor whom you know was really there when he came."

This was said with such indescribable earnestness that no one was aware of anything in the chapel except that Father Happé was telling them something.

"He can cure those who are sick even unto death. There was a priest I knew in France who was dying of a great cancer. And he wished, before he died, to say nine more Masses to the glory of God. He could hardly stand...it took him a long time and great pain...and each day it was more and more difficult. But his doctor would not forbid him, because there was no possible chance that he could live, he was so terribly diseased. And as he was lifting up the Host for the last Mass, suddenly he was made whole. There was no disease in him. And he is working very hard in his parish now, and that was many years ago.[1] With God, life and death are both so easy. We must suffer, otherwise we shall not have any share with Our Lord. But to have learnt not to be afraid is to triumph over the world. We shall suffer what God chooses, and die when He chooses, and what he chooses will be best for us."

Before they realised that he had finished, Father Happé had come down from the pulpit. He gave Benediction, and then they were alone in the church without him.

1. This is a true incident.

The curious thing was, no one wanted to go. Some went out soon after the end of the service, but they hung about outside. When at last Father Happé came out of the porch, they felt defeated. They had waited to say how sorry they were that he was ill, and here he was, grey-faced certainly, but laughing, with his arms full of mewing, wriggling kittens.

"It is for Leonora!" he explained. "It is her birthday, and I have asked Father Guardian that she may have one, and that she may choose."

Mrs. Forbes-Chippenham got into her motor with the buttoned-up expression about the mouth that meant somebody had offended her sense of what was right and proper. The car moved off round the circular drive, on its way to the gate.

"Oh," screamed Leonora, "one has got away!"

She was down the drive as fast as her legs could carry her, after a yellow striped kitten.

The motor moved slowly on.

Leonora was on the bank, grabbing the disappearing kitten. Then everything happened so quickly that it was only by dint of talking it over and over that everyone could agree about what happened. One moment she was on top of the bank, and the next she was running down, and the motor, taking the curve below, could not see her. She was running and not looking at the path below, but at her mother, calling that the kitten was caught! And something brown shot past them all, and everyone was deaf with the cries and the screech of the brakes. And Leonora was wriggling out of Father Happé's arms, sobbing that the kitten had run right under the car.

"No, darling, it is quite unhurt," sobbed Myra Garden. "Run and get it, quick, it is running into the yard, don't let it get away."

Leonora was off like the wind, quite unaware that anything had happened, except that people had made a fuss and she wanted to get the kitten for Father Happé. But when she came back, he was not there. He had had to go in. She would see him another day.

It was next day when they lifted her up to see Father Happé again, for he had been dead when they reached him, untouched by the motor, unhurt, with so great happiness on his face that all the village came to look at him and would not leave him. And the portrait which has made his face known all over the world was painted that night by Roger Campbell. It is not the portrait of a great archaeologist. It is the portrait of an old Savoyard Franciscan in the hour of his triumph.

THE END